Little Did I Know...
Thus Sonia Speaks!

Sonia Patnaik

First published in 2020 by

Becomeshakespeare.com

Wordit Content Design & Editing Services Pvt Ltd
Unit - 26, Building A -1, Nr Wadala RTO,
Wadala (East), Mumbai 400037, India
T: +91 8080226699

Copyright © Sonia Patnaik
Editor: Joan O'Brien
Illustrator: Aditya Raj

Thank you team BecomeShakespeare :

Pranali Naidu
&
Shreyas Prathamshetti

ISBN - 978-93-90266-07-4

Dedication

To you Tinku, for I know you are watching over us and smiling
my guardian angel. My buddy and my brother,
I love you through eternity !

Foreword

Little did I know

The collection of poems by Sonia represents a fundamental theme of human world —love.

Our meaning to life is given by love which can be exciting, emotional, inspirational and at the same time sad and melancholic. Sonia elaborates lucidly this fundamental theme of life through these poems vividly, with emotions and feelings as if these feelings are arising from her own experience of life as she demonstrates with a phrase, "Thus Sonia Speaks !"

While reading the poems, one gets the impression that the love which is expressed here is more than human, it is spiritual and spirituality connects something larger than human world and furthers our relationship with others.

Some of the poems very effortlessly relate to the overall theme of love and unfailing relationship through touching story like in "Red Ribbon Tree" where, the Princess and the Warrior fall in love, separate through misfortunes and reunite after a long time with same emotion and excitement and cherish their reunion — an unbreakable love.

The poems are written in simple, easy to read language which conveys the meaning of love, spiritual or earthly, to the core of the heart giving a feeling of nostalgia and perhaps a degree of satisfaction in life.

"Little did 1 know" by Sonia will be well appreciated by readers of all ages who would associate with the intricacies of both spiritual and human love and rekindle their personal experiences.

1 wish you great success Sonia for your launch and look forward to more in future.

Dr. Hare.K Mahanty
Retd. Academic
University of Canterbury
New Zealand.

Acknowledgements

To begin with let me be honest. Every word that I have written in this book would not have been possible if it was not HIM, the only Man I have ever loved!

But it was my Maa (mother) who taught me what love is. Her love transcends everything and she always loved me unconditionally. That is exactly where I see the other side of love and have been able to put it across through my writings.

And I pass on the same love to my kids. Waking up every morning with a smile is a blessing and it is my kids (Raj, Anuj, Karan and Mihika) who have made it possible. If not for you, I would not have known to love endlessly.

To the family I lost, to the family I love, my blessings from above.

They say love sees no boundaries; and the path to this limitless love, belief, faith and trust has always been shown to me by my soul sisters Nikki and Joan. Thank you for just being there forever!

Contents

The Child In Him — 11

Little Did I Know — 12

Timeless Love — 14

January Melancholy — 19

The Spring Child — 23

Forever My Sinner — 30

The Red Ribbon Tree — 35

Reasons To Keep — 40

I See You — 45

Just Shut Up — 47

Waiting for Your Answer — 49

The Lost Heart — 51

Thoughts of You — 54

Just Tell Me You're Fine — 57

A Fallen Angel — 63

The Truth Of Silent Love — 71

For A Moment Ever — 73

Somewhere Somehow   76

Monsoon Hues   78

The Bench under That Tree   80

Unfolding   84

Forbidden   87

Faithful Fate   90

Seasons for Reasons   92

Confessions of a Fearless Heart   94

Rain in Paradise   97

Frozen Heart   100

The One and Only You My Brute   103

You Are My Eyes   106

When Silence Is All   110

Thinking of You   114

Graceful Heart   116

Mysterious Love   120

Predestined   123

Tides of Tears   126

Sleepless Souls   128

Substantial   131

Sea or See   135

For the First Time   137

The One and Only Man in My Life   140

Why Do I Write About Love   144

Addicted to Romanticism   147

Flight of Freedom   150

Caged in My Dreams   153

The Wanderer   156

My Torrid Love Affair   162

My Bucket List   167

Believer   169

A Friend for Life   173

Across the Bridge   178

Unbearable   180

A Stranger Pretending to Be a Friend   182

Sinking into the Tide   186

Fate and Freedom   189

Penultimate Life   192

Alone I Shall Be   195

Nostalgia   201

Achievement It Is   204

Nobody's Fool   208

Funny but True   211

Unadulterated   215

Perplexed   217

Legitimate Hypocrites   219

Seize the Day   222

Hope vs Hopelessness   225

Deaf To The World   228

The Child in Him

I love the child in him
So innocent and so sweet
The mischief in his eyes
Those blushing cheeks
The tender way he spoke
Showed me that he cares
The touch of his warm hands
The gentle words like breeze
The smiles that we share
That filled my life with feel
For when I am with him

I find the child in me...thus Sonia speaks!

Little Did I Know

Little did I know

Far from truth

Your faint voice could melt down my roots

That spur of the moment

Your look towards me

Turned out to be the most heart yearning

The way you looked into my eyes — unafraid

The world started thinking

How could it be

Two people as different as you and me

Poles apart as humans

As we could be

You have your views

I have mine

When we stood there talking

Time stood still

I am sure at one point

You were thinking alike

What on earth am I doing?

Is this me?

I have no clue
What's going on
Whatever it is
I had never felt so strong
That one look just turned into our destiny
You know me well
Is all I can see
You read my mind
Where no one dared to tread
You spoke to me and swear
You took me by a surprise rare
Well what do I say
There is so much to share
Something is brewing Something is blooming
It's only fair
We are not in a hurry
Somehow I feel
The stolen moments that you gave me
I will wait on and see
To more beautiful days and dreamy nights
Our love evolving right before our eyes
Needs to stand the test of time
Little did I know
It is going to be "WE"...thus Sonia speaks!

Timeless Love

Love, as we know is timeless

A well found lover is like straight from space

Everything about it is magical

No thoughts about tomorrow

Just today it spells

That very first time

That he looked at me

Little did I know

It will be love striking

The way he said he was in love with me

Turned my life into a beautiful sweet dream

We laughed, we cried and we lost our pride

Then came this phase

Where we realised

Whatever comes

We will be there for each other

Then came this uneventful day with tremors

Suddenly we were spoken about in all the wrong ways

It was made sure that our love vanishes

But we moved on to every one's surprise

Then one fine day

I was told to be agile

If I met him again

He would get killed or hurt

Without letting him know

I just kept quiet

He kept asking me

What's going on

All I could do is just keep mum

I kept myself shut

But was dying inside

Told my clan

Can't live without him

Show mercy towards us

To that I was told

You better forget him

I was hurt

I was crying my heart out in pain

After all it was my only love

Not a game

Finally I gave up for my clan's sake

Went and turned out as a rebel in rage

Life took its course

As we went separate ways

But our timeless love remained the same

For whenever I prayed

He was first in my mind

I had promised myself only till the day I die

He will be the first

I will pray for every time

For my love for him will always stay alive

I have seen the entire world

But none like him

He was always a gentleman

He never questioned me

Took all the pain

Still didn't say a thing

I have no clue

As to where he is

I am sure he's doing fine

Wherever he is

Should be happy with a smile

At times I laugh at my silly luck

Well, why am I complaining

It was God's rude shock

We were not blessed to be together

He lives in his world

I live in mine

Rest assured

I am sure just like me

He would be praying for my plight

It was his prayer I feel that has kept me alive

Our love so true, pure and defined

We went through it all in tormenting anguish

Now we just pray and weep the rest

Wish we could have done something then

Never mind

It was our sacrifice

We were to live without each other

But one thing God couldn't take from me

My love for him through time and space

Just one prayer

For this absolutely perfect man

Keep smiling and believing wherever you are

For I will come back to you

Surely in next life

Our timeless love will redefine time...thus Sonia speaks!

January Melancholy

A January morning

Life was regular as always

Me doing my chores

You doing yours

The day was beautiful and wild

When I first set my eyes on you

Something clicked and made me think

You are the one I had waited all my life

With each passing day

We grew fonder of each other

Every time we met

There was this feeling of peace

Have I known You since ever

My soul mate was walking to me

It was a feeling of eternity

I could share anything with you without a blink

And still be myself

Never a doubt

Not pretending too

The way you smiled made me feel full of life

There was something serene and calm about You

You made me feel just like myself

Days went by with us speaking through

For some reason or the other

Then there was this day

We fought over something petty

I thought that was the last I'll ever see of You

But then walked in my destiny

Suddenly something amazing happened

And took us by surprise

I remember we could not see into each other's eyes

We went speechless for a while

Wondering what happened

Guess, we were dreaming

Or had our little fight

ended up in the most unlikely feeling new

I would never forget the way I ended up thinking

Our hearts filled with love

Couldn't figure out

What was right

Although nothing wrong in sight

You had touched my soul

No one ever did

The nights and days felt the same

But nothing was same for me

Our love was the only thing I could see

The way you held me in your arms

Was enough to forget everything

The way you said, you love me

So pure, so beautiful

You made me forget the painful life

I had once seen

I see it in your eyes

The love you have for me

I realised you are no ordinary Man

You were a blessing

God sent across just for me

You have your priorities

But that does not affect me

Keep me in your heart

Hide me from this world

Tomorrow even if you don't remember me

I will always keep you in my heart

And love you till Eternity

Forever it shall last — Our January Melancholy...thus Sonia speaks!

The Spring Child

When I came into this world

Little did I know

Life is a roller coaster

And will never slow

Hopped adolescence

Skipped teenage too

Then came an age

Where I started through

A lonely journey

All by myself

Just a little family

And a couple of friends

But then I woke up one morning

Right next to your thoughts

Before I could think it through

Who are you

My friend or my soul mate

Why do you matter to me

You just took my breath away

To realise you are my fate

You had just not knocked the door

You made my heart think

Hearing from you a little something

Was my ecstasy!

When did this happen

I swear I have no clue

But now my entire world

Had become You

I have fallen like a snowflake into the arms of the earth

Turned into a river

Flowing down to You

I thought falling in love

Was passé for me

Neither did I think I could

But when you knocked that door

You took my heart away too

Here I am standing hopeless

Without a bloody clue

Life seems magical

With every move I took

It's just like I am breathing

Only for You

Where was this heart

For so many years now

I could feel it skip a beat

The moment I saw You

I lived once, loved once

Now I am confused

Whether that was love at all

Or it is the one I share with You

I believe silence speaks

A million words alike

Would you ever believe me

If I never told You

I Love You! That's right

For now that I am at an age

Where love is a feeling

Hardly to be expressed

From where I see

It's supposed to be understood

Why are you affecting me

When nobody else did

Maybe you are just like me

The loner who lives in fears deep

I had locked the key to my heart

Thrown it out into the blue

But destiny is the real God

She gave you the key

And you walked in through

I dread the thought of love

It's not very inspiring

But when I see You right in front of me

There is nothing more exciting

You brought in so many moments

Just with your sweet nothings

And when I hear your voice so deep

It never fails to amuse me

You, the real you, nobody really knows

But You opened up your heart to me

We were two broken hearts

Once scattered with bitterness

Now that we have each other

There is nothing more miraculous

Than the nearness of you

Today I pray with my eyes closed

There is nothing more I need

Than being in love with You

Since the day you walked in

Faith walked back home suddenly

Hope I heal your painful heart

With my gesture of comforting words

I don't promise you the world

But my love I can assure You of this

I will love you with all my heart

Make You believe in life too

There will be a day

When we share our worlds together you'll see

Never will I make you feel

You could have been better

We'll have a home

Filled with love and its treasures

For everyone to see

Every soul that crosses our home

Will swear that we are lovers they have never seen

We have gone through the grave

And started to live again

Let's show the world

What love means

Now and forever

There is nothing more I wished for

Than being with you

Every step I took so far

Was nearness towards you

I don't believe in screaming out

Announcing that we are lovers

Our love so silent

Shall be proof enough to see

There's no one who would love like us ever

I could go on and on

But I guess there's no need

Love is better demonstrated

Than in a scream

Thank You my love for walking in

When I had lost hope

You just made sure

That I could love you fearlessly

Forever and ever

You brought back the spring child in me...thus Sonia speaks!

Forever My Sinner

There is so much I wanted to say

But writing down makes more sense.

We once believed our love was true

But then there was this reality check

Even though we love each other

This world is known for different troubles to make

With all essential flavours

Only if you could call my name

I swear I wouldn't look back again

Why is this emotion so strong and strange

We are ready to give up everything in its bargain

The best thing about love I say

Is we realise when it ends

The way we once loved

Just vanished forever

Without making sense

You are the one

I waited for more than ever

The way you loved

Turned all my wrongs to right savour

I'll be waiting for you hopelessly

Through days turning into nights

Waiting for you endlessly

Without letting go

Hoping in my heart

You will come along

Even if you wouldn't

Don't let me know

I'll wait and wait

Till the day I grow old

Even on my deathbed

I will wait for you to call out my name

Just for that one moment

When you will say "I love you" once again

Again in my next life

I would be born the same

I would continue loving you

Through the storm and pain

There will be a day when God finally decides

Enough of this hypocrisy

We were meant to be

Till death do us part

Through eternity

After all the bitterness

I have seen

Since the day you came through that door

We felt the sense of security from ages unknown

God was thinking about us when He created love

Let's put it this way

It was His call

He decided to make us fall in love

No matter how we deal with it

We were meant to be

No one but only you sweetheart

Can't you see

Hold my hand

Look into my eyes

Scream out to the world

"That's my girl," yes she!

People wondering out of shock thinking

What a rare delight to see a sinner realising his dreams

People if you are shocked that I love a sinner

Without any questioning

I will stop praying and start behaving like a sinner too

I have lost my world of rational thinking

The only thing that stands true for me

The sinner who loves me

The question my rational mind asks me

My heart gave way to you

I don't know the answer

Guess love has its way to you

Why I love a sinner

Not a saint instead

I shall remain loving you

God forgive me

I am a lover

That's all I have learnt to do

When my sinner turned out to be the only truth

He came into my life

Tumbled it alright

But all I have to say

I will love my sinner with all my rights

I do

Love doesn't end because we don't see each other

Love stays to see us back together

Forever my sinner

You shall remain my only true lover...thus Sonia speaks!

The Red Ribbon Tree

A little walk down the beach

Lived a sweet old lady in a lovely cottage free

Under a blossomed tree

Every single day she walked out

To tie a red ribbon on that tree

All of the village thought she was crazy

The least they knew of all

Was this woman's history

She was once the most beautiful girl

This world had ever seen

Now her greying hair wasn't shining

This lady so simple and down to earth

Never spoke to anyone ever before

One fine day as she was tying the red ribbon on the tree

The little children playing there came down to see

A little girl asked her "old lady what's your story?

Why do you tie a red ribbon everyday on this tree?"

Finally the sweet lady now with weak hands

Told her and her friends "come along children.

I am old now, so I will share a fairy tale."

There was a beautiful princess most fragile and delicate

She was unaware of this ruthless world

For she was kept safe and away

As she grew older she got prettier by the day

She was always surrounded by muses taking care of her the entire day

One fine day her kingdom was struck by the cruel King of terror

Every thing was broken

People killed and slaved forever

The princess in her tower high was next targeted

The first man to reach the tower was the best known warrior

The moment he saw her

His heart belonged to her

The scared princess crying in a helpless state

Asked him to kill her

Now that he had found her

The warrior without a thought said to this lady

Please don't get scared of me

For it's too late already

I am the greatest warrior this world has ever known

Never knew my heart could beat until I saw someone

And that someone is you

My lady for your heart is untouched

The princess was shocked to see a warrior talk of love

She could not believe her heart would respond to this call

The warrior took her hand and asked her to move quick

Told her he'll keep her safe wherever it shall be

She for the first time had trusted a total stranger

Her heart told her to trust him even if it meant danger

He took her away from the castle through the back door

Far away from her kingdom known

From the war to a new shore

He built her a beautiful cottage under a blossomed tree

He made sure of everything that she needed was provided
and seen

Their love blossomed in no time

The world stood witness to it

He said they would get married and settle right where they lived

But before they could take the vow

The King's men found the warrior's track

He hid the princess from the men

And asked her to keep a promise no matter what

Told her to tie a red ribbon on the blossomed tree unfailingly each day

For you never know when I will be back

I'm not sure yet

But tie the red ribbon

It will mean our love will live

Little did the old lady know the whole village was there listening

The men, women and children were crying all the same

So now you know people why I tie the red ribbon on this tree

He loves me till today

And hence I am waiting for him

For he is my faith

It was my love's gift to me

Dear people I am telling you this as I don't know what will be

Today I am speaking

But maybe you will never see me

Just then, hold your breath! There was a strange feeling

An old man was walking down through the street

The old lady stood up

Feeling her heart beat

Her warrior, her love was walking home finally

Was it a dream!

The whole village was shocked to see how the lady reacted

A woman who could barely walk was running towards him

Suddenly when the two met there was a moment of silence

The warrior hugged her tight screaming out

"My love my princess"

Your love kept me alive as you never broke our promise

The red ribbons on that tree is proof of the vow you keep

Our love for each other has crossed the barrier of grief

Now we are back together for all the love we missed

The people standing watching them were crying out their hearts

Timeless love unconditional vows

How immortal could that be

The princess and the warrior till date

Tie a red ribbon together on the blossomed tree of faith...thus
Sonia speaks!

Reasons to Keep

Have you ever sat down

With a reason as random as this

Why are you still smelling the air so free

The coffee that you drink

Reminds you of something or somebody

Who could be thinking just the same

Why are we stuck in that old game

When that little reminder of how you laughed

Could be the only reason to keep

Moving in this weird world had never been easy

But, you want to be that "in thing" always in the groove and jive

Like staying in the crowd is your kind of move

That's fine

Then your lonely heart knocks asking "where are you"

You pretend to be on the go

Always on a winning spree

But then again, your heart's crying

Stop it you freak

It's good to move with the world

That's your forte to be

Have you ever wondered

If that was really your incline

Was that what you had wished for

Each counting day you get busy

Doing your best for the world

The funniest part of it is that

You have forgotten what you were chasing or looking for

Sit down my friend

Slow your pace

Take a deep breath

For there are so many reasons to keep

Your awesome heart

That's at stake

We get what we sow

And reap our part

But, Is your heart content with just what you seek

We are running in the game of life to achieve it all at once

Let me ask you one thing "you still haven't stopped looking for"

Basking in the Tuscan sun

Smelling the air fresh

I know it's your retirement plan

But baby are you there

Walking hand in hand

On the sea shore is a dream that is yet to originate

For me my friend

There is no such dream

I believe in doing it all

Without any vice or whim

I may not be a tycoon in the game of life

But I know you can't beat me

When it comes to living right

I am a dreamer

Who dreams with her open eyes

I don't believe in tomorrow

So I move with today's light

I refuse to listen to a heart that lies

You could join in and see

The wilderness with me

From the race to the mountains

To the depths of the sea

Hold on my dear friend

Tell me your dreams

Make me believe you

Once and for all

I promise I'll give you

Plenty of reasons to keep

We just live once

Make the most of it

Wake up like a fresh flower

Not like a dying tree

Every new leaf should be your life's view to see

Just because you are in pain

You don't have to grief

For remember my dear friend

When you are crying out

It's only you who goes through that tormenting truth

And when you are smiling

The world smiles with you

Come on, let's walk together in the paved path en route

Laughing at our silly mistakes

Washing off our pride

My friend

Trust me life is so much more

Lets take the road to rise

And walk back even wiser to strike

I promise my dearest friend

You will never feel more alive

We will have so many reasons to keep our memories, fun and crazy times

Then when we finally retire from our lives

Our legs barely moving

You will thank me for it all

And the reason we were meeting

Let's live our lives in a way together

We become the reasons behind our lives forever

Then when we are finally gone

The world will walk our path undone

For we would have given them all the reasons to keep up with... thus Sonia speaks!

I See You

When there's a moving cloud

With the wind rushing in through

I see you!

When life takes a breather from its random tasks

I see you!

That moment when you turn your back on me

I see you!

The moment when you want me back

I see you!

Those times when you hold your emotions dark

I see you!

Then that time when you cry alas

I see you!

Point is I have no clue as to why

I see you!

The only thing that stands to be true is

I see you!

I don't give a damn to the world about that

I see you!

Every minute my heart skips a beat

I see you!

After all I got in return for being fair

I see you!

Damn it! When I hear your voice

I see you!

The way you have made me feel so far

I see you!

Somehow shows me there's no holding back

I see you!

Through all this and more coming up

I see you!

Does not matter who says what

I see you!

I love you as a matter of fact

Hence, I see you!

Waiting for you to see you back

I see you...thus Sonia speaks!

Just Shut Up

Sometimes when I think of you

I wonder if I love you or hate you

Ever since you were gone

I tried hard to forget you

Each time I try doing that

Your love filled eyes pull me back

Consistently to keep loving you

I don't really have a clue

Why on earth do I love you

You were the one who left me alone

Shouldn't I hate you from my soul

My foolish heart keeps calling out

Your name keeps ringing without a doubt

I keep forgetting all the while

How miserable you made me feel

From the first kiss to the last embrace

Memories of how we loved flashing back

Is it so easy to just walk out

You certainly love me with your heart and soul

I try calming myself down

Thinking that I hate you

My heart bounces back

And asks me to just shut up...thus Sonia speaks!

Waiting for Your Answer

You came into my life

Loved me like nobody ever did

You made me feel like a woman each time

Crying out with pleasure in my soul deep

Awakening my senses of sweet surrender

The first time our eyes met

There was no reason to talk or tell

Love spoke and we listened

Everything that was unsaid

Your subtle way of telling me

This is how you made me feel

I was born to be loved by you

Calm down my dear heart

Now that you are gone

I know it wasn't easy for you to walk out

When the need be

Come back to me my heart recalls

Then comes a knock on my door

Unimaginable to a fault

Holding onto my heart and last hope

I walk opening the door

My eyes pop out in surprise

On the contrary asking me

He stands there questioning

Did you ever truly love me

Almost fainting to his words

Shocked and confused I hear it all

He's actually telling me

He loves me like no tomorrow

Quote unquote he spells out

I have been waiting for your answer...thus Sonia speaks!

The Lost Heart

Contemplation where have you got me

Imagination is playing its game spree

My heart that was once cold and frozen

Has now brought in spring with flowering

Raging and pounding like a free bird

Loving in kind

Who could have thought

Your magic has worked

Can't you see

I am out of words

Violations of boundaries

Logical thinking has taken a back seat

The heart I was once afraid of

Has finally agreed

To lose myself in the middle of these mysteries

I don't care if I don't know what love means

Loving you has been mesmerising

Everything is making sense

Things are now transparent

Tried to hold on

Not to dwell in

But again the unstoppable me

I laugh, I cry and I keep thinking why and when

My heart just had to beat

When you were crossing then

It's such a delusion

My forsaken heart

It saw you coming

I hadn't figured that

Your eyes crushing on me

Your arms soothing my pain

What is this feeling

Overwhelming, procrastination my distressed and tired heart

Kept wondering till your beneficent self touched at last

No it's no more a dream

I live you the way I love

Stopped questioning myself sometime back

You stepped in without a knock

Never to leave again

How unfathomable, this piercing truth

It's a decisive warm pain

Loving you unconditionally is what I have to do without prejudice

It was always a fact

You loved me all through it right

Just the way I did

I Love You that's a pivotal fact you see

For I shall live and die with you in me

How can I ever thank you for finding my lost heart

When you ask me what have you done

I thank you for finding my once, lost heart...thus Sonia speaks!

Thoughts of You

Can you ever love someone

With timelessness and beyond

Between two different worlds

With a feeling so passionate

Your heart gets misplaced

The tone of his voice

Sounds like your heartbeat without choice

You feel his arms around you

When he's nowhere around you

You feel his lips kissing yours

Never been kissed is the word

You hear him say I love you

Whispering in your ear at night

A love with such conviction

The universe conspiring

Passion and wildest dreams

Coming alive in the scene

Resisting this could be possible

You turn it away in fear

We had never known such love

For this I could take heartbreaks

A million times and over

For I have known forever

It's temporary in nature

If we allow it to be

Just one moment in our lives

My life, my passion and my feelings

I would risk it all in this dealing

Without remorse or regrets

Saying you are mine

To deny such a love would mean

The fatal of mistakes

If we don't live this love

Turns to injustice in itself

A love that is spiritual at heart

Never physical misleading

The love you wait a lifetime

A love so strong

Neither heaven nor earth

Could stop it from being

Now you know my one true love

Why the thoughts of you are killing...thus Sonia speaks!

Just Tell Me You Are Fine

In a world full of fakes

There lives this friend

Who wants to see you fine

To any extent

Even when you move on

Don't remember her name

She just wants to know you are safe even then

For she was your friend before you could know

Don't take her for granted

Please keep it slow

She never judged you through these passing years

Stood by you through happiness and tears

She was the one who warmly welcomed you

When all of the others

Thought you are insane

All she asked for is a little acceptance

She never went beyond than being your best pal

You forgot her in the glittering games

She kept quiet and took it in her stride

Believing that you were alright

One day when you came back after reigning the world

She was right there

Standing, waiting for your call

She never questioned you

Why you never thought of her

Rather she was happy

You were fine

Wherever you were

You kept telling people, Oh she's my friend

She can wait for me

Till I don't see her again

She kept her pain hidden from this world bitter

Couldn't declare to anyone

How mean you were to her

She spoke about you

Always the good things of course

And all you were talking about

Is it a favour she's done

You are a go getter

You believe in taking the ocean tides

All she keeps praying for is

Hope you are fine

One fine day when you had lost it all

She opened her arms

When the world closed all doors

For she had been your friend even when you were gone

Waiting every moment for your return

You took a lot of time

She never complained

Well that's the basic difference between friendship and pretence

You told her how tired you were from the way you were duped

She held your hand and told you

Are you fine, tell me the truth

She asks you, if there is something that's disturbing you

You can't hold back and start unfolding

Crying like a baby

You have forgotten where you have been

She cuddles you up with her shivering hands

Feeling your pain

Crying along with you

Trying her best to console you

Then when you ask

Why hadn't she kept in touch

She pats your head telling you

You had never gone, not once

Finally when you are in control

Back in form

She softly asks you

Are you doing fine?

You are amazed at her words looking surprised

Telling her

You were missing her silly advice

She laughs out loud, as to why you said that at all

And you turn back and tell her your all

You dumb girl, can't you figure out

I went through this world with my bravado and was proud

End of the day, I am back with you

I was searching for someone who might be like you

She's all in shock as to why you said that

She's just an ordinary girl with no one to match

All she wanted to do was

See that you are fine

She gave you your space

And kept that in mind

Then there was this little awkward moment

In a fraction of a second

You have found your soul mate

You hold her tight

Right in your arms

Telling her

Listen you silly girl blind

From today you are only mine

I was a fool

Who for all these years

Had travelled through the globe

When you were right here

All she says is one little thing

I always wanted to see that you are happy and fine

That is when you realise

What you could lose

If not her

Who else would you choose

Your life is now just around her

That vague little girl had become your gift after all

All you want for the rest of your life

Is to make sure that she is loved forever fine...thus Sonia speaks!

A Fallen Angel

Long time ago, there were two estranged lovers

The girl had her man running all over

She wanted this and wanted that

Made her man chase all over the mart

One fine day when the man proposed marriage

She asked him for a gift which was beyond human courage

The man was dumbstruck as to what she just asked

Confused his mind

With what he just heard

Did the girl who he loved so dearly

Want a fallen Angel really

Before they could marry

He kept wondering what he would do

Finally he started for this unforeseen journey

Wondering where on earth would he find a fallen Angel

He went around everywhere

Just to find if it's possible

Keeping in mind

If he didn't find a fallen Angel

He could never marry his childhood sweetheart

Not now or ever

Then, finally, he got a clue

The place he would find one

His dream come true

Well it was equally a funny trance

A fallen Angel could be found

How extraordinary his fate was around

Happy with the fact that luck was shining on him

He ran to the place where it was last seen

All he saw was a pair of broken wings fallen on the ground

And his heart sank further down

Right there was a lady sitting in a white gown

He ran towards her

And asked her with a frown

"What on earth are you doing here lady"

For he thought that she had taken the Angel already

To that the lady in white spoke out

"I am a fallen Angel, you man with doubt"

He laughed his heart and spoke out in tempo

Are you mad

You crazy little lady

I am looking for an Angel certainly

Not some lady

Please don't tell me you dropped down from heaven and your
wings broke already

She then said

"Could you please help me"

She had hurt her toe when she had the fall

The man then reacted with anger towards her

Sarcastically yelling you are an Angel really, Ha ! Ha !

And from your fall you just broke your toe, not bad

He was a good soul

Thank God for that

He helped the lady to rise up

He took her in his arms

Sat her down near a tree

Then he moved to search for the Angel frantically

Tired he came back and sat next to the lady

What am I supposed to do

The Angel is gone already

By then, this pristine lady in white

Was glowing like the moon

In the dark of the night

She then asked the man

"Aren't you the one who made a wish"

That a fallen Angel is what you seek

To this the man just stood up in shock

How do you know what I had wished for

For nobody, but my heart knows only this thought

The lady sitting there smiled with grace

Well your love made me fall

Straight from heaven's gate

You silly man

Can't you see

I am the fallen Angel you seek

The man was angry

Out of patience by then already

Replied back in disdain

"Don't, fool around me lady"

I could take that joke

Some other time maybe

She then said with her gentle voice

Yes, why not when your silly girlfriend wanted a fallen
Angel

Why didn't you ask her then about her whimsical wish

The man confused

His brains bursting out

He told her

If you are an Angel

My lady shine like one

For a change maybe

She stood up

Shining so bright

Almost turned the world to light

And finally when the man was convinced

He said to her

Well it's fine, I will take you along

Consider yourself my wedding gift back home

Then they started the unusual journey

The lady walked along without questioning

Finally when they reached home

The man went into an irreplaceable shock

The woman he loved was standing with another man unknown

Telling him the same thing she had told him once

He bursted out crying

For he loved her with all his heart

And she had treated him like a passing phase just like that

Just then the pristine lady in white

Asking him if he was alright

No! he shouted

Can't you see, all that I dreamed about has shattered into scatters within

Then something out of this world happened

Unheard and unseen

The Angel with her calm dispose hugged that man

And then she told

My dear man, I am a fallen Angel

I had fallen for you

Not for your lady unstable

I saw your honest heart

So filled with love

Wanted to know

How is the feeling of it all

So when you wished for a falling Angel

Without thinking I took the leap

You have taken my heart

Can't you see

The man was surprised with the words he just heard

An Angel had fallen for him in this human world

Gaining back his confidence

He moved to that girl

Holding the pristine Angel's hand

Look here, you wretched woman with hues

I have found an Angel and look at you

You are a witch with a thankless heart

Hence, God gifted me with an Angel from so far

She loved me from the farthest of sky

And you couldn't know

What is to love being beside

Well, what an irony

You keep your men

And I get to keep my love for once

My Angel from heaven has loved me since time immortal

I am going to love her all my life and never falter

Well, what a blessing in disguise

Loving an Angel is not in everybody's life

Now he and his pristine Angel are man and wife

They are still in love

Glowing each time

Love can be a miracle true

For you never know

Which Angel has fallen for you...thus Sonia speaks!

The Truth of Silent Love

Have you ever heard about

Silence that speaks

Yes it's called silent love

The one which never screams

The love that stays in your heart

It's that feeling of being complete

The thought of being perfect without perfection

Those eyes that have been speaking for a while

And the lips are sealed without a kiss

The feeling of ecstasy without you touching me

That only moment with you

Which we have never ever seen

The union of two pure souls without touching skin

Words that are understood

From the distance of two worlds

Our hearts longed to see

For love as we know is beyond these fields

Love is always patient and kind

It is never jealous or malign

Love is never pompous nor undermine

It is never outrageous nor selfish nor unkind

It does not take time to know who's the lover

Love takes no pleasure in other people's sins

Rather takes delight in the truth unseen

It is always ready for acceptance in total

And to endure whatever comes says the lover

My silent love speaks

Nothing at all

Just keep your love

And keep loving me throughout now and forever

For we are gifted with the silent love from above...thus Sonia speaks!

For a Moment...Ever

Have you ever felt for a moment

The thoughts that cross my mind

Any moment at all was your heart ever mine

A moment where you were perplexed

Wondering what it could be

A moment of your nearness to me

Whether it was real or just a dream

A moment that defines our destinies

When I sit down to think through the darkest of nights

There comes a moment of silence that makes me cry

Were you my friend ever or an enemy, or a traitor behind

A moment that we had

Could be well-defined

But you left me in the moment before I could take a call

Each moment these eyes that shed tears for your words

Are they the only moments when I pray for you

Ever in your life did you have a moment when you spared for
me too

A little thought about me even in despair

You lived in those moments

And the moments lived in me

You left in a moment without announcing

I waited every moment for your returning

It's a waste of time but I live the moment each day

Hoping some moment you will surely come by

These moments I have spent waiting for you

My soul mate you are my moments

My tormented heart knew

If ever any moment you come back

Make sure you're not late

As I am running out of luck

My eyes will be waiting for your welcome in kind

Don't ever blame yourself

For my soul left that very time

The day you came into my life it was to love each other

If you ever for a moment could feel the love through me

Spare a little moment and bring some flowers for me

For the moment you left was the day I left this world

Here I am! Yes this is me in a picture frame

A moment captured in my candid best

A smile on my face framed and put on this desk

Waiting for the moment

When you will bring my moments back...thus Sonia speaks!

Somewhere Somehow

For a lifetime it has been a dream

Longing for someone somewhere somehow unseen

There has been a phase where everything made sense

Then there was a time we ran out of patience

Life is such a delusional mystery

It never fails to mock

The bitterness it left around in an astounding shock

Who wanted a life so cruelly unfair

Now that we are dealing with it

Does it matter anyways

When was it that we last laughed

Do I remember why?

In the strange pavilion of life's unassuming match

Did I see a little light or walked the dark path

Somehow my short-lived happiness of being with you

Turned into mourning without much ado

You were gone

So were the dreams I had conceived

Convinced me to confirm that it was all a myth

I believe that change is the only constant

So follow the rule! Somehow I wait for the change itself

Consistently I wait for that particular point of view

Somewhere someone dares to dream my way too

My friend, break free from this ordinary life

Do the extraordinary with that impossible dream

Pursue it, follow it, chase it down

Live for a second

Does it matter all around

For all you know it just might be the eternal truth

Somewhere, somehow, someone is just waiting for you

My dear friend, for all the trouble you have been through

Trust me this very moment blessings are smiling down at you...thus Sonia speaks!

Monsoon Hues

Ever since the day I have known

Monsoon happens to be my favourite season of all

The first rain drops that kisses the face of earth

The scent of earth suddenly transforms so magical

Like a hopeless heart that has waited for years

For it's love to pour out the essence of tears

It's tragedy and romance both facing fear

The story of two estranged lovers

Who have waited long years

To meet finally after God's intervention

When the first shower pours his heart out

His lover starts blushing

Without hesitation or doubt

He's all out there shouting his love profound

She smiles proudly stating poise astound

It's amazing how two fateful lovers

Meet only once every year

She never complains

For she knows him well

What's love other than miraculous patience

Only shows that love is not time bound

It stays strong even after a million years and still counts

One thing that the lovers showed me

Every time it rains and touches the earth

Somewhere someone is falling in love for sure you see

Through the monsoon hues of time

I stole a line

Yes it's love and absolutely fine...thus Sonia speaks!

The Bench under That Tree

On the sea beach serene

There was a bench under a tree

An old couple walked down there

Every evening with their love and glee

They sat there talking about life and tragedies

The old man always had his arm around his lady

She always leaned on his arms without feeling guilty

I used to hang around the café

Writing my mind free

But every time I saw them

There was a sense of belonging

They shared the same cheer

How extraordinary!

I wondered looking what would happen to me

Its such an amazing feeling

And was a rare sight to see

Two people so much in love

After all these years

Could it really be?

I made it a point to visit the café everyday if not writing

Just to see them there

I was fascinated each time I looked at them

Until one day I couldn't hold myself back

I walked down towards them

I just had to ask

When I reached them

There was the warmest welcome I could have asked

The old man said "come and join us dear"

The old lady without a thought said "sit down my dear, have a beer with us oldies, without fear"

In no time we were enjoying each other's company

But my crazy heart was getting uncontrollable

For I just needed to know everything about them

What had kept them in love so stable and flamed

Finally I asked the couple if you don't mind

What has kept you so much in love through all this time?

To this the old lady replied promptly

Oh! Sweetheart you have no idea

Let me tell you about it

I have held on to this old man for fifty odd years

I was amused at her answer so sleek

Felt like my generation had never taken a leap

Then this fine old man said

Listen my dearest girl I'll tell you a secret tonight not shared at all

This old woman has always kept me preoccupied

She's one demanding wife

And I am no feeble man

We have kept it going for so many years by now

As we never fell out of love

Rather fell in love with each other each passing day

To this I said

Where do you find such commitment today?

Suddenly the old lady took my hand

Holding it gently said

Listen to this my young lady

There is someone in this world

For when he comes into your life

You will surely be struck

To this I laughed out my heart

Hadn't the slightest of clue

The couple then said

It's about time for our march

And off they walked through

As I saw them walk

Some thing just changed in me

Years after that moment

Here I am with you

Sitting on the same bench under the same tree

Repeating the old couples' magical love story...thus Sonia speaks!

Unfolding

Never had I ever imagined

This moment that's gradually sinking in

I take a step towards and then hold back

Wondering what's intoxicating me

Is it the wild rain or is it the smell of you

The cloud messengers are showering me

I can feel you around me

Passions roaring through

Or is it the Gods simply acting cute

Your presence is all around like the air I breathe

Yes those arms are exactly where I want to be

It's been so long

The thought of being complete

Want to hear your heart beat in proximity

Is it as furious as my heart's beating

Holding hands walking through the beautiful fields

Sitting under a tree laughing endlessly

Painting dreams that are gradually coming in

We understand each other without questions asked

You look at me and get your answers too fast

Power of silence is what love is

There is nothing to speak

It's just you and me

Our hearts are unfolding gradually

Should be that way I guess

No one's in a hurry

When two hearts start beating as one

Ordinary transforms to extraordinary stance

One look and I know what exactly you mean

Fearlessly I pave the path along with you

I know the hand I am holding will never mislead me

I am sure this is what I have been waiting to see

Your warm touch ensures you will stand by me

We could sit through for hours just looking at each other

You make me come alive by just a soothing smile you see

It's love or do we have a name for this feeling

The way you are an over-grown child

You want it all or nothing at all

I didn't know what to do earlier, but now I am sure

This is exactly how you are going to be

To be honest I love this child likeness in you

Annoying yet astounding

Clueless what to do

Never ever did I think you would be like me

We seem to have forgotten the world

It's just we

Whoever thought that we would be together

Was certainly sure of this

We are made for each other you see

Well it's actually "mad for each other" that is how it is

Unfolding ourselves we are together

Let love do the speaking

And let's lose ourselves in each other...thus Sonia speaks!

Forbidden

When I wake up every morning
Hearing the birds sing melodies lovely
The sun unfolding through my window sill
Clouds send in messages through the cool breeze
A familiar smell awakens my heart indeed
Was that you next to me
Or your thoughts rebounding
Can't figure this one
Everything is alluring
Incandescent I lie on my bed
Finally I am living
Everything is beautiful now
Turmoil of unwinding
Never was I sure about this overwhelming feeling
When was all this falling together
Is this called weaving
I have forgotten time-bound stress ridiculously annoying
Our fingers entwined together

There's barely place for breathing

I have never been so sure

Phenomenal and inspiring

If this is love what we feel today

It has surely been defining

What could possibly be more perfect

It's pointless improvising

A moment that we spend together has brought in life amusing

The mellow tone of your words sweet, indeed promising

Nothing can replace your love

It's with me in my breathing

My heart you took

My soul compelled

Bowed down to you in giving

I couldn't do a thing about it

My mind had stopped thinking

Your chaotic heart was meant for me

You said it confirming

We laughed out loud

We cried and fought

Only to be back rekindling

You always kept your faith in me

I kept it all in sealing

Let us be the way we are

Never in disbelieving

When you can trust someone with life

You have all your meanings

And then when we are too engrossed in our love confiding

Suddenly there's a knock on the door

I wake up to it screaming

I soon realise I am back to life

I am forbidden to be dreaming...thus Sonia speaks!

Faithful Fate

Amber is the colour of the sky tonight

Ocean tide rising high

Blood moon makes its move to state

The colour of love is indeed red

My hazel eyes are burning bright

For the wait for you has ignited alike

The wondrous feeling of moments wild

Have turned me to destiny's child

One look from you has the power on me

Melting my stone heart to feather-like feel

Tried hard not to analyse a thing

Never believed in mourning

Each time I moved away from you

Your thoughts compounded like musical moves

Lightening striking through

Every time I see lovers in arms

The only thing I think is you at once

When will I possibly belong to you

We are dreamers or fate has a play too

Had always heard hatred blooms into love

Does love bloom into hatred too

Well either ways you take it

Love and hatred belong to the same group

You can't hate someone if you have not loved him too

You possibly couldn't hate a stranger, could you?

What is it that binds me to you

The more I want to hate you

Love is making its smooth moves

I see, I smell, I breathe you

Tried too hard to cheat my heart

Somehow it seems to find only you

Finally I gave up and figured out

Loving you was the only thing I was born to do

No remorse, no guilt, no pride to be

My faithful fate has taken its control

I am as good as dead without you

My love, it's a fact my heart shall beat only for you...thus Sonia speaks!

Seasons for Reasons

When we start to understand life

Decoding its mystery and delights

The first time we heard our heart beat

Was a reason how we saw the season seep

Every season has been a reason to feel amazed

For spring is when our love is in bloom

All colours filling our life

With the future that's so true

Summer makes us realise

It's not an easy walk

To be successful in love

One has to walk on fire and be back

Monsoon drenches us with the overwhelming power of love

Making us complete together forever and ever to come

Sealing the bond of promises

To have faith on each other

Then walks in Autumn teaching us life has its ups and downs

For if we don't face it together

It will only get difficult around

We face it head on

As we want this bond to last

Mighty Winter walks in

To play the last dance

Even better we say

It's the ultimate season of romance

Walking through snowfall hand in hand

We have finally given all the seasons all the reasons to keep

Loving is not in everybody's book of feels

Be fair, be honest

For you never know

The reason behind your love could some day become immortal

As long as we are around now

Let's leave our reasons for seasons now

To let the future lovers come and see...thus Sonia speaks!

Confessions of a Fearless Heart

I choose to be

You may call me anything

From a woman of misery

To the soul of a lioness

From the queen of drama

To the epitome of silence

For the reason behind your anger

Or the answers to your prayers

The outburst of your mind

The sigh of your heart's fate

The million times you misunderstand me

To the billion times you care

The reason for you hating

The reason why you love

That one time you touched me

The moment that time stood by

From the people who speak against me

To the people who know me well

The countless days you didn't see me

To the memory you left back here

From being the quintessential woman

To the woman you took for granted

From where I thought you betrayed me

To my unconditional love

You took for granted

For my being the woman available

To me belonging to none

For my suffering you will never know

To my heart that belongs to you but none

Forever I shall love you

And you are not aware of

Or don't have a clue

My fearless heart that cries out

Silent confessions of my love true

My love I will keep loving you

Does it matter after all

I don't need no mercy

My love still stands tall

For you my love will never know

What's to love fearlessly ever at all

Yes, I live and I will love you

Till I seek my dawn

Come here and stop me if you can

I shall lead you to the confessions of a fearless heart you see...
thus Sonia speaks!

Rain in Paradise

The weather Gods have taken a call

It's time for a moment of mystical fall

Heaven's happy singing of love

Drenching the earth like never before

The thunder and light illuminate my fate

Like droplets falling on my face

The smell of earth soaking in the water

Invigorating in all its fervour

There could never be a fine metaphor

To merge love and rain together

It's an hour of total

surrender

Fall in love or be gone forever

Twilight trails the breeze that chills

Only a heartless brute could oversee

The lonely heart that has waited a while

Will see a smile

From the light coming from a mile

If only you could grant permission

I will keep your heart safe in all conditions

The feeling so over-powering has taken its turn

For it's just not moments

It's life as one

I shiver down with the thought of it

Are the God's crazy

Or is my heart deceased

I can surge the essence of what befalls

Never my mind who could have thought

Now I know the complete plot

In the matter of heart

There is no mind

It's unconditional

Unthoughtful yet strong

Where the heart has been longing

Mind is lost

When the yearning hearts meet finally

Gods are smiling down similarly

For this is the day which has been awaited

Two hearts as one shall beat relentless

Breaking the rules of this illusionary world

Rain in paradise

In the valley of love...thus Sonia Speaks!

Frozen Heart

Lost in the arms of thorns

Long enough to withstand the storm

Burning helpless without a thought

Life and its rude side

Just pile up

Dreams turned into nightmares deep

No promises, no memories to keep

Treading path them screaming in pain

What a price to pay for love so sane

Losing everything I owned forever

I have no tears left

My eyes are dry now

Longing for you has left my side somehow

Love for me is just a fancy name

It's nothing but a preposterous bloody game

There is no one worthy

No one I can trust

The flowers have fallen and thorns are cast

Piercing catharsis to burn in hell

Heaven does not exist

It's just a tête-à-tête

God changed His address and forgot to tell

Foolish me was waiting

For an answer from nowhere

I loved so truly

The Gods would have wept

For today I hate everything that comes close to me next

Stopped believing in miracles

Only reality barks

I can only do wrong

As that's my new right at last

You took away my love

I didn't say a word

You drowned my faith in my own blood

I stood there watching

Couldn't do a thing

Today it's a different me you are seeing

I do as I please

Don't believe in anything

I am as good as dead

I don't feel a thing

There's possibly nobody I stand a chance of belonging

Committing the oldest sins in the newest of ways

I learnt the trade of this world and its traits

When I hear people pledging their vows of love

All I do is walk past

Not interested at all

Yes I am alive

I breathe and live

Practicality is more pivotal than fantasy for me

When I am questioned about what I feel

All I answer in return is

My frozen heart has forgotten to beat...thus Sonia speaks!

The One and Only You My Brute

I'm not very sure of what it is

That pulls me towards you

I'm not the kinds

Who lose their heart to random normal kind

I'm just a wandering wind of soul

That comes across once in a lifetime

I'm sure you think

I have lost my mind

When it comes to define

I'm honest enough

About how I feel when I'm with you

Trust me enough to know the truth

It never struck my mind

I'm the one who lost my heart

While trying to fix yours in time

I'm the one who drives you mad

Loves you beyond time

I'm sure you are going through this feeling new as well

Wanting to break me down

In your arms swell

I'm sure you are as clueless as me

When it comes to us

I'm not very sure

What you would feel

If you found me in the nearness of your heart

Would you let go of me

With just a little look

Or make me yours

All the while through

I'm so sure you will love me

The way you hold my heart

One thing I know for sure

I can't escape that

Why I'm in love with a brute like you?

You make me feel alive

Just by looking me through

It's complicated

I know what you are going through

Believe me I know the truth

My heart has given up when it comes to you

It's all on you to decide

What's that you really want to do with our love this type

I'm so sure of my heart

It can't beat beyond yours

All I have is a waiting heart

Not knowing where it goes

One thing I can assure

It's not going anywhere until you come too

Take your call and let me know

Whether I befit you

There's no man who could ever match my brute

That's you, my only truth...thus Sonia speaks!

You Are My Eyes

When you look into my eyes

I see myself in you

You were born to love me

They speak to me too

Sparkling like wine

Intoxicating!

When you whisper to me

Telling me you go weak seeing my eyes

My eyes speak back to you silently

No words spoken yet well defined

Sense of belonging has taken its stride

Who would dare to look at me

When you are residing in my sight

Only you my love so kind

None but you

I have no time for anything else

When you said "you are mine"

I live you

I breathe you

I feel like your sunshine

I feel like a woman when you smile

Only a real man has the power to derive

A man who's a woman's pride

When your eyes touch my heart

Time stands by

There is no other way

To make us feel alive

You complete me

When you look into my eyes

My prayers are answered

Now I know why

Who could possibly pick

A flower from the dust

Hold it in his hands

Never to let it die

Not everyone has the strength

To go beyond time

Wonder why I was kept away from you all this while

Or is this the first time

I know what love means otherwise

The wait has been worthwhile

Your love has proved

Miracles still happen

In this world full of cruel

You are my love

Allow me to flaunt my life

The love we share is rare to find

Dreams and hopes

You have put across my life

Are more than enough

For one lifetime

I could love you for ages

And still not be surprised

You brought in a faith

I had lost for some time

Finally I see myself

Not alone in my life

Your love has moved

Heaven's doors in time

Shaken the walls

I once despised

When you are with me

I become more than sure

Who could have loved me

But you my dear

When a man has the ability to love a woman

With only the way he looks at her

No words can define that sacred union divine

Only Gods would know the reason why

Then when you tell me

My eyes are your life

I look down and smile

Only because

You are my love

You are yes my eyes...thus Sonia speaks!

When Silence Is All

After a point in life

When you've witnessed

A journey to hell and back

You sit down to analyse

Things from your past

Well you tried your best to save it all

But somehow things just kept slipping out of hand

People came in claiming to fix all of that

Few could see the pain you have seen

Trying to convince

Never came easy

There were a couple of odd souls just like me

Who saw the truth and believed in me

Not to forget the treasured ones who stood by me

To an extent they went all the way to see me smiling

While I was trying to assemble life's strike on me

How can I forget you all who came in

Right when everything was going wrong with me

Some kept it rolling by

Sending me memories of my favourite places I have been

One old friend I have

Flew in so I could see

I can count on my fingers it's exactly three

Who kept me going

Even when I was tough on them

They kept telling me there's more to life even today

I am tired now when my own have failed me

Where could I possibly be

I swear I tried

But this world is so full of lies

I am breathless now

This hypocrisy chokes me

When I cried you guys kept me going with your tricks

But now that I know

I fail to see

I don't know who to trust

It's a far cry for me

I have responsibilities

Or I would have preferred to die

It's just a body

My soul has left me long back

Can't really relate to anything not anyhow

Void is all I can see

Everything is meaningless

Nothing is real in this superficial space

Never ever am I going to ask who, when and how

For what I have seen is enough

Can't handle it, not now

When my peers broke my faith

What is left to think of

I am broken

Couldn't see it coming

Shattered! My heart doesn't beat anymore

Don't want to speak to anyone about anything

God failed me long ago

Now humans do the same

I'm not shocked

What a blessed life

Will a thank you just do?

I will not say a word, not anymore

No more ever will I ask, pray or love

Never will I hear from anyone even when they try to speak

You will wait to hear me out someday I seek

What can I say when silence is all I picked...thus Sonia speaks!

Thinking of You

I have been thinking of you

The way you make me feel

I am scared now

For these feelings feel so surreal

I always thought as to how it felt

But was never sure of it

I cannot falter now

I have to hold onto You

When our eyes are locked

It's so hard to escape you

When you leave me and go

I so want you to stay

There is so much to say

So much to hear

But for now I'll just keep to myself our truth

I want the world to hear too

Love doesn't fear anything or anyone

The love we shared over these days

Strong yet true

Can't believe it's happened

Only if we had a clue

At times, I want to scream it out

Those words I have kept within

They explain the pain

The fire within

To the failed attempts I have tried

I am clueless

How long I'll keep these thoughts

Thinking of ways to do

Don't know where to begin

Amused and confused

What to do

I'll just let it be

And wait to see

It'll happen if it's meant to be

I have your love

I have your heart

And it's tearing me apart

Just want to be with You

My soul keeps thinking of You...thus Sonia speaks!

Graceful Heart

Grace a virtue is very rare

And rarest of it is a graceful heart

You are this "alpha" man

You have got it all

Don't need a reminder

The way you run your world

Women falling for you

And trying to woo you

Man! You are one helluva guy who has it all

The money, the pace, the unlimited race

You have got it all through time and space

You love to party and laze around

Your so-called friends using your account

And there comes this passive phase

You are almost broke

And pretend to be rich and fake

Your bank accounts screaming "we are empty"

Then you realise you were living a lie

The friends you called family are growing faint

You are sitting alone in your old rocking chair

Analysing what you did

Wasted your life in vain...

Then you remember this strange girl

You once called her your friend

And never had the time to sit and listen anyways

For she had foretold your future back then

You just overlooked saying "Oh that's faraway"

She was your friend when you had none

And today again you are standing alone

She had warned you about this doomsday

You were in your spirits right over the moon

She had asked you to hold on your breath

You were busy playing life games

From this girl to that

You were never sure

There was a major confusion with your way of handling life to endure

Today you are done with your million friends

They ran away and now have no time to spend

You are contemplating what you have done

In the process you have lost it all

Living a fake life was your call my friend

When you didn't listen to this genuine girl

For she was telling you the truth and guiding you through

Yes her name was Grace

Now you remember

She always spoke the truth

And in silent surrender

Today when everyone you knew is history

Grace is with you to solve the mystery

For her heart is pure as pious as she is

Never promising you unnatural things

She believes in prayers

And God listens to her

Grace she is and her identity is love

When you say "I Love you"

She says I did too

It's just that she never spelled it out

Made you wait to realise and see

She's Grace

She's a virtue very rarely found

Now that you found her

Don't ever look around

For she'll give you a life of completeness

With your confidence back and your life back alive

Better treat her right as she's the only one

Who stood by you when all others ran

Now that you both are together forever

Love the graceful heart and become a believer

Yes you are smiling and will do that forever

Grace and you are perfect together...thus Sonia speaks!

Mysterious Love

A little mystery could be more of an attraction

Than putting it all out there or giving it away

Blind instinct as they say

You just know it when it comes

Free from momentary distraction or impulse

I honour my authentic self when I choose

To protect my vulnerabilities without compromising virtues

I know that denial can't hide truth forever

What justification could you possibly give

When you lost your heart together without a wink

I thought of it as a passing phase

But then mystery of my heart had me chase

You don't need a year, a day or two

Just one moment and it's all there to prove

How silly have you been

Not to confront

Just a glance had taken my life into your hands

Is it a secret that you had kept all this while

You loved me and never acknowledged in pride

Mystery shrouds me

As now I am in your arms

The fear of losing had never been alarmed

Till the day you kissed me on my forehead

Love is a clichéd topic now

Very random and free

What has then cast its fog on me

I couldn't possibly derive

What is more mysterious

You or me

Or maybe the warmth and tenderness that we feel

Why is this yearning to know it all so reckless

To know what is it and solve the mystery selfless

Your smile makes me feel happy from within

Your anger troubles me and willingly I take your pain away
without guilt

Your silence kills me a million times and over

Your happiness means happiness to me

Incomplete without you is what I feel

And still can't solve the mysterious feeling I feel

Who are you?

Why have you cast a spell on me?

Your mysterious love is killing me...thus Sonia speaks!

Predestined

You were a stranger

 So was I

The moment we smiled at each other

Well, there was a reason why

We were predestined to be friends

Before the beginning of time

Whoever thought we could plan our moves

Was definitely ignorant of this fact

Our friendship was never time bound

Right from the start

Our relationship will last a lifetime

Through the sands of time

You and I never knew

It was coming to us

Now that it's here

Well that's no surprise

We live and love being together

Spending our time doing nothing at all

Just in our world of complete surrender we reside

Laugh, cry and fight without a reason or clue

Two insane people were meant just to be through

For anyone hearing out our topics will faint in shock

How can two people talk nonsense

I say "why not?"

And make sense out of it all

Well insanity is a synonym of friendship we say

That's what we friends have decided

Maybe it's not in the dictionary

So what !

Anyways we don't want it

For me my dear friend

You are the only truth if you see

When the whole world walked out on me

You were the only one who walked in

You took my hand and said "damn this world

don't you worry buddy I'll never let you fall"

My buddy my dearest friend

I had promised myself

There and then

No matter what happens you shall always be

My best friend in this world

Who never judged me

Who never questioned me

We accepted each other

With our bad and our good

Our bonding of friendship is nothing but the truth

At least we don't pretend to be in someone else's shoe

However insane and crazy we are

We love each other

That's true

The best part is we don't dope or drink

Our togetherness has given us a high on life with dreams

We promised never to say "thank you"

Too formal for us

One warm hug means a million words

My friend my lifeline

I was never fine before that

We were predestined to be friends

Like no one else could ever have

Life was never the same till you spoke back to me

Our friendship was written by the predestined...thus Sonia speaks!

Tides of Tears

My boat from its familiar place

Somehow got untied

The wind swept it away

To an unknown ocean wide

My heart bleeds with the tide of tears

In the river of sorrow

Filling it up to the brink

From bank to bank

Other boats of life go ahead

Prepared to embark

I stand light bedazzled

Bewildered in the dark

Desire to lose one's way

Withdraws one further far away

Time to roam directionless

Through the deepest of nights

Lost in the arms of my beloved

Like dusk murmurs to the night

Low, sweet syllables of serenity

Draw cool kohl in the Sun's red eyes

Soothe its hot gaze with sleepy eyes

Let the raindrop kisses spill

And thrill the earth with pleasure deep

Soak the greening secret saplings

Hidden within each tree

Awaken their rich leafy lives

To blossom joyously

It rains here round the year

Cloud herd here like deer

Parasite tendrils appear

Cling to doors like wattle

Melting hearts in distant quest

In aching sleep

I seek solace

Again the midnight knock

Flaming, piercing and yearning skies

Towards the tides of tears ride...thus Sonia speaks!

Sleepless Souls

One very precious thing

Is a good night's sleep

With peace within

There are people in this world who are blessed with it

Then there is this other category

The sleepless souls who dare to dream

With their eyes open all through the night stream

It's strange no one can tell

For they have not slept

For ages at stretch

Only they could tell

Why they did so

Whether they slept

Or spend the nights through

You see these sleepless souls

Are a little distinguished from the outside world

They don't intrude into anyone's zone

They belong to another world altogether

No I am not talking of zombies, ghosts and spirits

They are humans who eat and breathe

It's just that they were misunderstood

A normal person would never have a clue

Sleepless souls are always on search

Who could understand their delicate hearts

There are so many of us who belong to that group

It's an absurd thought

But it's true

Some of us really get to think it through

What keeps you from going all out and being like them too

Why are sleepless souls considered insane

Just because we live the utopian dream

If we sleepless souls weren't looking for details

This world would be full of people fake

We have our own rules and regulations

What the world thinks is just an illusion

We live a life too

Brutal and factual

Don't believe in fights for years and years

Sleepless souls are divinely pure

We might not sleep

But our hearts do rest

Well it's not a very pleasurable nest

But we are the ones who see your pain within

We became the sleepless souls

Out of choice not deal

As we get to find what we are looking for

To all sleepless souls out there

Keep on with it

Exactly this way

For the way this world is evolving

There are a lot more there

Who'll start rethinking in a few more days

Following the trend we have set

Making sure

Everyone's hearts rest

Yes, we are the sleepless souls

Join the club or let it go

Finally you will see one day

Being a sleepless soul

Has never been easy...thus Sonia speaks!

Substantial

Amused by the fact I have been observing

Inculcating the thought of how you see me

You don't have to prove anything at all

Loving me was never mandatory in your list

There is never a moment when I don't think of you

It's not important at all

You do the same too

My love for you has never failed me

Irrelevant of the fact that you don't know the real me

It's not necessary you should feel the same as I do

I take pride without prejudice in loving you

It's been there since ever

Overlooking all the consequences that came through

Love happens

You can't force anyone to love you

That very moment when your heart takes over your mind

Why this phase of anticipation that you find

It's the feeling of being complete even when you are alone

I have learnt to live with the fact

What's bothering you

Weaving lives together was never easy

You know that too

Some of us are meant to be alone

Yes I am a loner who loves fearlessly

I don't think it's anyone's business anyways to judge me

No conditions apply

No dreaming high

Let me be is all I can sigh!

I have a promise to keep

A long journey to meet

I maybe a worthless heart

Well that's how it is

My peers think I am wasted

But respect me for what I may be

My love for you is so steady and strong

They have tried hard and given it up

Bowing down to my thoughts for how I love

Silence can mean a million words

It's strange you couldn't see

Not your fault

Not in a hurry nor in haste

I am not waiting

And you are not late

Your silly tricks don't affect me you see

I am way above these petty thoughts trust me

Harmless as I am

Commitment is my virtue

You will never know that I love You

I am not very verbal about my feelings profound

I wish and pray for your well-being around

I fail to understand why I do so

What makes me do this when you have made me a joke in town

Well someday you will fall in love and get your answers right

I will not be around to witness it all

That will be the day when you will know

Why is it important for something substantial

My prayers walk with you

Now you know why

The day you find love like this

Do confide

Hold onto it for you never know

I will love you through life and beyond

Don't ask why You

I can't explain

I am sure you know now

Not everything has a reason

After all it's not a game

My love for you will stay no matter what

Substantial enough to win the world...thus Sonia speaks!

Sea or See

The pleasant sea reminds me

I had just begun my journey happily

To meet the horizon of my deepest dreams

Like the sea filled with a million mysteries

Only if I could see what it was showing me

Instead I sat on the sand

Counting waves free

One by one my life came walking around me

The first wave I saw was when I took my first step

The second showed me the many things I have been blessed

Third time it was a high tide

Just like my untamed heart

Fourth and fifth made me laugh

At the silliness of thinking that

Those were waves of expectations

Which didn't work for me

Then I noticed the serenity of the universe

Where the sky and sea meet

That's where I saw hope, faith and love at their peak

Suddenly everything fell in place indeed

Enigmatic thoughts were out of the plate

As a free soul

All I did was waving it off

I figured out you were perfect

I loved you profoundly

The waves finally taught me

I know now that you are imperfect like me

And my love for you grew beyond me

Overwhelming!

Could this be happening to me

This is the longest time

I have sat by the shore

Contemplating our lives

Why is it so

Thankful to see the sea

In its natural best

As it could be

That's when I realised

Did I see the sea

Or the sea saw me...thus Sonia speaks!

For the First Time

Life gives me a million reasons to forget you

My heart gives me only one reason to stay

Through infinity and beyond

We came together tearing apart ourselves

We gave us our gift of love

For the first time

May I give my life to you for the first time

Can I leave my loneliness behind for the first time

For the first time

Can I fly and float in profundity

For the first time

Can I be born again

Will you not meet me in the eyes

Just like our first time

Wouldn't your lips seal mine

The way you thought about it for the first time

Our sweet nothings

Till our eyes met and time stood by

For the first time

Like a saint giving in to salvation

For the first time

Our hearts being mended

Oceans apart

For the first time

Like a muse without sleep

My thoughts strive hard

The soaring pain in my eyes

Cries to my heart

For the first time

You being harsh has not worked on me

Don't even try

As you will see

Those piercing words

Turning into lotus petals

Falling all over me

For the first time

I now know the pleasure in my veins

For the first time

In a state of ecstasy

Everything I see becomes you indefinitely

This state of constant melting probes deep in our souls true

This feeling tormenting us

For the first time

This minute torture is playing with my life

For the first time

What could be more blissful

Than feeling your touch

For the first time

May I give that hug

The way you wanted to hug me

For the first time

Love knows no reason why it's there

When we least expect

It's just there

For the first time

You and I prove

Some things are meant to last for a lifetime

In a moment of truth

For the first time...thus Sonia speaks!

The One and Only Man in My Life

People did I shock you

Announcing a man in my life

Please breathe my friends

It's not a shocker

I am not talking about a man who walks the streets alright

I am talking about the only man that exists

He is none other than

The seeker of divine justice

You know Him well as the ruler of our world

He's a trickster

The ultimate truth of all

In this world He has a lot of names

Call Him God

Yes He's a priceless gem

Also known as Shri Jagannath Mahaprabhu

Let's put it this way

What's in a name!

For me He's the only eternal truth

I love Him and hate Him in equilibrium

He's my Man and my joker too

For when I meet His eyes I start crying

Before realising why I do

We have been in this arrangement ever since I was born

I was born on the day of His favourite game of all

He coloured me the day I touched this earth

Yes, it was Holi, the festival of colours

I tell you

I hate this Man for His dark sense of humour

My pals tell me

You insane girl

You have the audacity to call Him your Man

Why not I keep saying

Why can't He be my man

If He's not bothered

What are you freaking at

Just because of our relationship status

I don't play Holi with any other

You can't fill a cup which is already full

Nope never!

Since He's coloured my heart

I don't need any colour to run through that

He's a prankster

His favourite game is life

Look what He's done to me

And still manages to smile

For when we both are together

It's confusion at its peak

Some ask me whether I love Him or hate Him

They ask me to please be decisive

My only answer to them is

Love and hate walk side by side

You can only hate someone if you have loved Him with all the rights

Well, He's my only Man through the hemispheres

Does my crazy world sound delusional to you

For if you ever knew Him You would feel the same too

The moment you look into His deep button eyes

Your heart will skip a beat

And you will be in love with Him

Trust me on this

I love Him openly

Never a feeling of shame

For He's my only Man

In heaven and in hell

As well as in between...thus Sonia speaks!

Why Do I Write About Love

We live a life full of assumption, presumption, confusion,
devotion, faith, hope and trust

One thing that is common here is a heart filled with love

Assuming life with love

Presuming it could be love

I write about love

As I fail to understand the concept of it all

That utopian dream I have always heard

But never seen

That cloud without a silver lining

Or is it a cloud at all

We say we love our family our friends and peers

Why is that we stop by just to hear that one name so dear

Well it's beyond repair

Can't be deciphered or decoded

But surely there is some reason why we fail when surrounded

I am a daughter who loves

A sister who loves

A friend who loves in semblance

Most importantly a mother who loves nature's creations that are priceless

But when it comes to loving a man unconditionally

Well it's beyond me, whatsoever

Maybe I am afraid

Or is it that I can't trust

Does it exist at all or have I been told so

I guess when one sees the pain and prerequisite demands

The heart stops to reason for something so mundane

There is more to life than going through it all

Possibly I was born free

And do not follow worldly laws

I am a rebel, yes!

And it's great to have an untamed heart

Well at least I don't go about playing games with someone's feelings

I fail to understand why one would dwell in at all

You can only be useful to others if you are true to your soul

Allow the light of awareness to spread its wings of fire

Why is it so important that one person makes all the difference

When you are surrounded by so many people who love you for

who you are

Is it really required to fill in the social norm just to make you a star

You belong to this world

Well certainly not the idea

We are at times a little insensitive to the idea of living life wisely

What's good for you could be bad for me

Give it a thought kindly

Add space to your thoughts and let be

I am sure you will find there is lot more to life

By simply understanding

There could be a whole new world of better not bitter life awaiting with delight

Just the way you like

Gave enough reasons as to why I write about love

I could go on rephrasing

Love sure wins through the universal truth of the Divine ... thus Sonia speaks!

Addicted to Romanticism

Since ever I have been hearing stories of love

Let's keep it simple

I am a romantic at heart

It's human to look for things one hasn't seen

Well I am one of them who's just heard of romance

Never felt its essence

Not overlooking the fact of defiance to dream

To fall in love with the concept of love

Being in love for real are two tangents well thought

It's not easy to be ridiculed over being in a situation

When you have no clue

Whether it was love at all

Could put you in humiliation

Coming to the thought of romance

Well just a thought crossed my mind by chance

How magical it would be to just hold hands

Speaking through the wee hours not blinking once

Entangled in each other's arms

The feeling of warmth

The sense of security at once

Clueless to the world

Our wild hearts dance

Sparkling eyes of you and me

Can light up this dungeon of our unruly grim souls set free

A walk together by the sea

Could anything replace it

Reading each other's mind without saying a word

Well, romance is all about being comfortable

That's all

The moment when my heart skipped a beat

Was the time when you looked at me

How blissfully connected we soul mates

Nothing has ever been more perfect

When you hold me tight and give assurance

You are there

What were my chances

Ecstatic is the feeling of love

Knitted together are two dreamers with one goal

Two hearts beating as one

The onlookers are turning green with envy

Shocked at our intimacy

That we are "We"

Companionship and compatibility are rare you see

The only thing that exists between us is transparency

We don't lie

We don't cheat

Just love each other piously

You came into my life when it was crashing down

Held me up without a frown

Showed me the power of faith without risk

I promise today I will never let you down

Even if it means staying apart never to meet

The trust that you have bestowed on me

Will stand through time and the world will see

Love is not just being together

There is so much more

And I will remember

We always were made for each other

I belong to you

I am addicted to romanticism

You gave me a real reason to be this way

You do...thus Sonia speaks!

Flight of Freedom

The air is pristine, pure and kind

Never was the feeling of breathing freely so awesomely sublime

Life finally has given me a trillion reasons to live

A billion milestones covered

To bring back the real me

My silence of dignity has brought in gifts and how

I might have failed God somewhere

But He has always been kind

Everything is beautiful now

Even the weirdness undefined

For the ones who stood by me and those who were unkind

The people who care

And the ones who laughed at my pain

I have no words to thank you for believing in me again

No matter where we go

There are a few without who life is not liveable

Vanity as a virtue has walked out of the door

Never to knock nor to bore

Sanity is back and well

I am sorted

No more pretending

No more in the hide

It's not a moment that I live for

Nor am I in love with my life

One can be good without being perfect

It's just a lifestyle

I gave up on my perfectionist goals

Hence I am not bothered

Who cares if everything isn't "just so" all the time in order

The little imperfections in life

Are what make it so interesting

A smooth camouflage of veneer over everything

Isn't impressing

Emotionally it's not real

Intimidating and overpowering after all

It's a sign

And it could be putting walls between us you know

Break the walls down

Leave a little message behind

For it's just the beginning

Not the end after all

Reflections of you in me

How could I not know this anyhow

Always thought I could say anything at any point of time

Contradictory my heart and mind

Fighting each time

It's difficult to speak when I meet your eyes

Thought the only thing I have now is indefinite sacrifice

But it's my love

I have learnt to live with it through time

My flight of freedom is empowering me to reach the divine

You are not my past nor present

Neither future well defined

You are me

Just me cause my soul is still alive

Forgive me

For that's how it's going to be for the rest of my life

People call me a loner

Little do they know

You are always on my mind

Flight of freedom has taken its sail

For you shall always be

My be all and end all...thus Sonia speaks!

Caged in My Dreams

Not long before I learnt to fly

Fire of freedom with my love so fine

Lost in my life

The world was new again

Bright and beautiful

I was reborn

My faith and trust were back from the dead

God's play was not over yet

How could He be so kind to me

Not yet

Sent His best messenger to be kind to me

I thought it was the most amazing dream

Only to be shattered

In no time you see

My wings were cut before I could realise

Faith was crushed

And trust was walked upon by

How could I trust again

For it doesn't exist

It's a lie

I was just a means

An object to be played with

As I sit down to contemplate

What went wrong

I realise it was a nightmare

Not a fairy tale at all

Well after all this

With my broken heart

I preferred to forgive

To let go of that

I'm back in the valley of darkness I belong

Never to see light of the days to come

Caged in my dreams of despair

I will never believe in God

Or any of His ways

Caged I am

Caged are my dreams

I caged myself yet again

Threw away the key

Never for you to find me

Caged in my dreams

I barely breathe...thus Sonia Speaks!

The Wanderer

I have a friend — this globe trotter

More of a mad wanderer

He kept searching the world for his lost treasure

Wow, how clever!

On the hill tops

Through the mountains

And down along the sea

He kept searching everywhere

Without a reason to cease

His search was unnatural

As he kept searching absurdly

He's still searching for some destination unknown

A path that he treads free

Think he enjoys the journey

More than his pain to heal

A long, lonely soul

My heart goes out for him

Hope he unravels his mystery

Before the world sets him free

He has been a crazy wanderer

With no direction to flee

Something he completely forgot

Everything is predestined

No matter how we search

There is one destination to reach

Assuming procrastination

You finally end up where you have to be

No rules, no reasons are right or wrong, dear wanderer

No matter if you go across the oceans three

You will be a loner

If you don't know what you are searching for

We often say the journey is more interesting than the destination

Well that's certainly true!

But when you don't know what you are looking for

How long are you going to search

How far would you tread

You will reach your rightful place

Only when you are not looking for

Let life surprise you

What's your hurry

I am sure you will find it one day

It was right on your floor

My friend dear wanderer

Why are you always confused

Have you ever heard of the saying "what is meant to be will be!"

You transformed from a young boy to an awesome man clean

The thing you forgot is now you are not in your teens

When your youth withers into the seasonal fall of youth

Have you ever realised who will be your friend

When you're old and lean

Who will tell you sip some coffee

Or take a little walk

Maybe you have locked your heart and kept it away in shock

But I am sure, my wanderer It's just a little vain

Cast away yourself into the tide that flows

Oh! I forgot to ask you

Do you know swimming at all

How about the kids you always wanted

But never came to this world

Stop wondering for once

And stop being a wanderer

How long will you take to realise your basic life skills

Working late nights has never been your priority

You have earned enough fame

Made the fortune you did

Is that all you wanted from this world indeed

You say you have seen the world

Yes I am sure

But did you really find dear wanderer what you were looking
for

Whenever I see you convincing me with your words wise

Something just tells me you are a loner

Wandering scot-free

If you are so happy with the world around you

Why can't I see that in your eyes when you are smiling too

When I argue with you about what I feel

Suddenly you start being defensive

My only hope for you my dear wanderer

Wish you find happiness

Right where you are looking for it

Your pain is tormenting me

Can't you see

Just in case you forgot

It's the same with me

The only difference we probably share

You kept on with your search and I ceased it before I started it

What worries me is not your search

I feel you are too blessed to go through these ordeals

Wake up! The roads never end

You surely can

Stop! Analyse your life ahead

Let me tell you one thing

I never shared with the world

Peace is within us

That's where it's found underneath

My dear friend my wanderer

One word for you

Let go of your fears

Some day I had gone through the same too

Live, love and trust are real words

Don't take them for granted

I am sure at some point

You surely wanted

My dear wanderer

My friend for life

Get back home to me

And tell me you're mine

Leave the wanderlust behind...thus Sonia speaks!

My Torrid Love Affair

It's been a while since I heard of love

Being in love was a far call

Somehow it didn't go well with the people around

They kept wondering how I could be happy and sound

Living alone for all these years

Untouched yet sane

People and their fears

I was their favourite game

Some said "Oh she's in love for sure"

And a few just made it very loud and clear

She's always happy and smiling

Too much positivity

There has to be someone in her life

How is she happy

The best part is

I was always the way I am

Never proved a point to any of them

Never had any plans

Then came this fateful day

A long lost friend

Came over to say a simple "Hi"

That was it to raise hell

One pure hello rang the bells

Some said I blush when I hear his name

Few actually saw us romancing

God knows where

I am speechless at misinterpretations of friendship pure

My poor friend ran to some island

I am not sure

One thing these feather brained people do not get

Common sense is seriously uncommon you bet

Why would I need any man for the matter of fact

I made a choice and I am content with that

A few jobless people who have no meaning in life

Are packing my bags to make me someone's wife

I am a woman absolutely ordinary

Trying to live peacefully

How easy it is to take a name that easily

What did one get from breaking a beautiful friendship

Or was it that we ordinary friends indeed are extraordinary

I lost a friend

Never mind some day he'll understand

What about you haunted souls

Hope you are happy in advance

Undaunted I am

Decisive is my path

I will, I shall walk tall

Try your luck no chance

You took away my friend

I never complained

You put me out in the world

You got your fame

You accused me of a torrid love affair

So what do you have to serve now henceforth

To make me feel like dirt and nothing worth

I am a woman who believes in herself

Surely not a damsel in distress

Tell me when you are done with your sheer nonsense

I have been laughing and I will do as I please

People who know me will always care

People who don't

I really don't care

Well through all this vagaries and jokes

I am waiting for my friend who will come back again

He's a fine gentleman who stays away from loops

Don't take his silence as his cowardice you fools

For the day we both are together

We will laugh at you

There is more to us than a few of you

Your curious thoughts couldn't do a thing

Everything changed

But our friendship remained

Your cheap tricks just didn't work on us anyways

Waiting for that day

When everything will be out in the open

We will show you what friendship means

Not every man and woman have a steamy scene

Alas! You desperate scattered brains

Your life moves around only under other people's names

How would you know that two people can be friends

To burn your flames

My torrid love affair remains

Hallucination is the word

Hope you wake up sane...thus Sonia speaks!

My Bucket List

A few things that I will do before I die

A little effort to dare and dream

A little power to touch my God I haven't seen

A sunrise from a window

While clouds passing by never been

A beautiful day where everything is pristine

A walk in the rain with you holding me

A bonfire on the sea shore on a cold winter night

A snowfall on the mountains at an altitude high

A bike ride to some destination unknown into the wild

A rendezvous around a waterfall nice

A million butterflies all together colourful and bright

A flower field through the horizon never-ending sight

A gondola ride through Venice streets

A camp on the Himalayan bed would be just amazing

A sip of wine from the vineyard of Spain

A lot of Swiss chocolates without gaining weight again

A full moon night in Leh

Can't wait to see

A cozy recliner to read my favourite books you see

A day to act mad like no one's watching

A day with my friends where I laugh till I weep

A day when I hold my mom

Hug her and sleep

A day with my siblings to relive the pillow fight and scream

A day when I see my kids become responsible men

A day when I know what is to truly love again

A day when I stand with my unconditional man

A day when I wake up in his arms hugging me

A day when everything is perfect and right

All this and more

There's so much to explore

I hope to live a little longer to see it all

A dream that's definitely going to come true

Hoping beyond hope

My silly bucket list drools

The priority of it all is doing this as "we"

My one and only love I mean

No matter what I will live to see...thus Sonia speaks!

Believer

Life as we know comes with a lot of gifts

We were blessed with plenty not to miss

Loving, living each moment as it came

Thanking God for most of them

Just when you settle down thinking all is well

Hell rises to remind you the devil still dwells

You do all you can to save what you have

Agony it is

Was never in your hands

Some things are meant to be

Date with fate has played its trick

You wake up screaming

This is not what you wanted

Realising that some things are better gone than granted

Your pleasurable dream has come crashing down

Whoever told you it was perfect

Made you a clown

Well, there is nothing possibly one could do

It's best to be alone

Than to be amongst fools

Do your worst!

Your heart shouts out loud and clear

Suddenly you see

You are not scared without doubt

Don't bother about people

They didn't live your life

Hold on to yourself with honour and pride

You are not guilty of anything

You have done no wrong

There will always be people who love you for what you are all along

They are the real ones who have seen you evolving

Stand by you

No matter what your surroundings

The negative parasites will soon realise

They are wasting their time

Honestly you heard me right

When none of their foolish trials work

They fall flat on their faces

And are laughed upon by all

One thing they couldn't ever do was touch your soul

It stays as pure and determined to the core

Unhindered your soul

Stands the test of time

My friend hold on for it's just the beginning not the end

Primitive are these leeches as their primitive brains

You were born to fight

And it shakes their roots off their demented brains

Pat your shoulder

Speak out honestly

Walk gallantly through these creeps

You can't mess with me

You petty losers

Move on with your high spirited self

No hesitation whatsoever

You were born to win

No one can rule you over

The conviction with which I spell it out

The only reason being

I am a strong believer

I believe it's about time I got my life back

I believe God walks with me as a matter of fact

I believe life from now on will be absolutely fine

I believe I am perfect with my imperfections in line

The quintessential permanence and truth

The believer in me believes...thus Sonia speaks!

A Friend for Life

When you are tired with the fake smiles you throw the whole day

There is someone in a corner

Who's hopelessly laughing away

When you come around to ask him why he did that

He simply replies "I was laughing at your stupidity you dumb lass"

Then he makes you feel like the silliest person on earth

And hugs you and tells you "What are friends for?"

You start laughing back

Telling him you are tired

He returns the favour by telling "You are such a liar"

Before you realise he has grabbed your hand

Tells you let's go party

The night is still young

When you try and give him excuses

Of how busy you have been

He promptly tells you

Just be a girl

You're not a drama queen

The moment you hear that

 You fight like cats and dogs

Suddenly he tells you

Let's go out have a ball

You argue needlessly

Of how tired you have been

There he's standing telling you

It's time for a treat

Whoever told you he will understand

Let me assure you

He's a friend and that too a man

A friend you could call at two in the morning

He takes your call without thinking at once

Asking "Is everything alright?"

If you are in trouble

He'll be right there

Standing with you all night

Holding you and ensuring

It's going to be fine

We choose our friends

Bring them into our lives

If you found the right friend

Well it's a blessing in disguise

When life takes you through steep rides

Confusion at its peak

He's the only one sharing your secret like concrete

People usually misinterpret their friendship as love

But what's the big deal

Indeed you love him after all

If you can't love your friend

And if he didn't either

You would never be friends

For any other reason seen

There is nothing more pure than a blessed friendship

The world will think whatever

You don't care

For you know where's your calling

The moment you had tough times

Crying out for help

This blessed friend was the only one who controlled your unstable state

The world talks absurdly

Well that's their job

They have no clue

You have your friend

Standing right next to you

You were strangers once

Now you are best of buddies

When he didn't care what the world said

Why are you worried

He stood with you in good and in bad

He made sure no one talks ill about that

Yes you found your soul mate in that friend you have

Keep reminding yourself

Friendship is pure

You in the world so fake

You found a friend who's dependable

Every time you are in pain

He makes sure it crosses him over through

Cherish this friend that you have found

For he is an Angel from God's chamber

Make sure you treat him right

When and where able

We have millions of friends

But there is this only one

Who will risk it all to see

If you are safe in your den

Comfortable as you can be

The beauty of friendship lies in dependability

There is someone in this world

Who makes you really giggle

The best part is while discussing the girls he's been dating

You fall off the bed with the faces that he's been making

Whoever said that a man and woman could never be friends

You're more than welcome to come and check our craziness

He's my best friend

My mentor and my guide

And certainly a man chivalrous as delight

But end of the day we are friends

That's what is all we look for

We have been friends since the day we were born

There is nothing I want more

A friend for life I did find

Awesomeness and beyond...thus Sonia speaks!

Across the Bridge

A million times and over I have come to terms

To take that step and see myself what life offers

The bitterness of yesterday keeps pulling me back

To go ahead and see what tomorrow has

Life has given me a chance yet again

To live, to love and pray

A major source of hope and find my faith

I am unconditionally getting pulled with what lies ahead

Suddenly all that was negative has moved out of the way

What I see today is a true blissful life

How amusing this feeling of completeness so right

Well-deserved break after a stormy life

Walking towards beautiful dreams at night

Living with anticipation of an amazing time

Yes! It's me can't believe but hey!

It's me for a change

Just me revealing to myself

Always thought what lies across the bridge

Never did I contemplate

I would find me

The bridge was always there solid and strong

Reluctant me was scared to take the turn

The hesitation has disappeared into oblivion

Today it's all me right here

If you can't love yourself

You can never love anyone

I am glad I took the call

Finally to discover the "ME"

Across the bridge was standing my destiny

Promises of life eternal and fulfilling

Take the leap my friend for you never know

You could just get lucky like me

There is nothing more rewarding than this

Across the bridge is where you want to certainly be...thus Sonia speaks!

Unbearable

Every person who walked this earth

Would have gone through the fact I talk

Why is it that I am misunderstood

What did I do that's so unreasonable

Did I show you the mirror of truth

Made you think and made you look

Your life is going astray and down

If you don't get what I am saying

Just look around every face wearing a mask

Talking big and acting smart

One thing you forgot my dear

Doesn't really matter when you reach the end

People who loved you

When you were a nobody

Are those few who loved you unconditionally

Cause when you are famous in the game of life

People will love your name, fame and vice

It's your call if you couldn't see a true friend

How far will you go with this self-obsessed gain

Time ticking from days to nights

Open your eyes and face the truth

How unbearable a pain have you left behind

Given the tears can you ever rewind

When you are tired of your vices and games

Come back to your old den

Unbearable for you this world shall be

Be sure you will find me

A friend who never judged you

I will make sure I will weave your heart

Then we can move on with a fresh start

Laughing, crying, fighting and still going strong

That's how we started our life, remember?

Stop torturing yourself just in vain

For when you say life hurt you

There's this unbearable pain that my heart regains...thus Sonia speaks!

A Stranger Pretending to Be a Friend

Have you ever come across a wannabe

He simply pretends like he's here to be seen

Whether you have it all to be his buddy

Well...As if!

Then when you give him a chance

He pretends to be your only buddy in advance

Talking and walking along like a freaky encyclopaedic

He behaves like he knows it all and well — you go blank

Like you are from the planet Mercury

An alien to his ways

Tells you he's a busy man

But is free throughout the day

Has everyone in a trance

You still continue to be his friend

Overlooking his boastful imbalance

Just when you think he's changing for good

Whoa! You realise he's a pompous fool

From the chapters of Cain and Abel

Suddenly your world falls apart

When you realise he's not your friend

But a minuscule part

He has been talking loosely about you and everyone

All your friends who have been there since ever

Start telling you

You could have behaved a little more wise

You are so very out of words then

Can't decipher why he played such a cheap game

All that is going round in your head

"What was I thinking,

I would rather be dead"

Your heart has broken into a million pieces

Scattered everywhere like flying leaflets

Why did I trust him in the first place

I was so happy without him instead

You had good friends

You always will

But this man came in like a pathetic steal

When you realise

The catastrophe is done

Every nook and corner is shouting out your name

Look at you

What have you done?

Trying to be a friend has cost you and how

All the friends you had

Always protected you

But, this pretentious man left no room

For as much as I know

A friend is a friend for all seasons

At least they don't pretend to be when you are a little distant

What a foolish man he could be

To overlook friendship like these

For the moment

My dear friends who are close to my heart

Stay away from this man

As a matter of fact

I took the blame because I didn't have a clue

But if any of you get hurt

It will make me inconsolable

For I swear on our friendship

For over the years

I'll make him forget

Pretending from this all new spheres

If you don't value it

Please step out

There is more to friendship than your pretentious doubts

And next time

If I see you anywhere around

It'll be your last day on earth you hound

Next time that you are back in this town

I will put up posters of you screaming out loud

"Beware of this wannabe

He's a stranger who pretends to be a friend

And then flees like a drain"

If you don't understand

What friendship means

Pray with your heart

Never to be seen...thus Sonia speaks!

Sinking into the Tide

There's something inside me

That's surely not right

Each time I look into this world

I'm taken by surprise

Confused at its pace

The world looks like a dim light

Each one of us is somehow living a lie

Some cry out loud

Some just sit quiet

Everything and everyone is raring to reach some height

Unknown unthinkable is the price

I lost my old world charm

Trying to figure out what's wise

Nothing seems good

No one can meet me in the eye

How unethical

How could you do this to me

Unthinkable!

Am I living a life

Or is death finally meeting me

Not sure what I want

Not sure how to break the code of uncertainty

Have been trying too hard

Only to swim across a mile

That feeling of drowning

Fear of losing

Everything I once epitomised

Pivotal moment of truth

When I look into the universe which lies

Does it lie to me

Or does it mean something

That I can't decide

I want nothing that life has to offer

Neither the truth nor the lies

Loving was my forte

Now I have forgotten that feeling of delight

Dungeons and darkness preside

Afraid of darkness

I always looked up for the eternal light

All I can see now is deceit, fake promises and elusive tribes

Good for me

Serves me right

How dare I think of goodness

In a world full of curses in scribes

Now that I wake up each morning

I start my day with a lie

Happy me, happy world, happier than ever, the sugar-coated flaws

Alas! My heart stopped beating

I couldn't agree more

For all I do now

Is wait for that one tide

My life is slipping through my hands

All I can do now is sinking down into the tide

Wishful thinking for yet another life

Free from these worldly ties...thus Sonia speaks!

Fate and Freedom

Rare little combination

Fate and freedom

One thing in common

It's their intersection

When both collide

That's when you know

What happens to your life

Fate can be derived as born to be

Freedom screams what you ought to be

Can't really let go of either as we see

One side is the world

On the other are we

Fate is the world

Freedom is you

Here steps in the enigmatic perplexing due

Do hell with the world

Or hell is we

After all the struggles of being alive

You finally see

I'm sure most of us have walked that mile

Well! Well! We still manage to smile

When all you want is to scream so wild

Tired of telling people

"Oh! I have never been fine"

Hanging out with people

Who make no sense

It's not easy to decide

Whether you are being fake or them

It's important to be in the crowd you see

Who cares if you are a loner

As long as you grin

Your soul is dead

It's easy to pretend

I'm in love with myself

I have let fate and freedom intervene

Where I take it from here

Totally my choice

Vice it is

Why if you wonder

Cause fateful freedom is like an addiction

I surrender

The world pulls you down with all its strength

You rise above

Making them go their ways

Forever wishing

I was born for this very day

Turned my fate into freedom without fail

If I'm a loner

I'm free to be

If I choose to be irrational

I will be

This is what you and you and you want to be

Turning fate into freedom

You finally breathe

Let go of the world

It will talk always

There's no high like being YOU

Whatever said...thus Sonia speaks!

Penultimate Life

It is said that only when we are close to death

We realise how important life is

Some words are forgotten over time

But some remain etched in our hearts permanently

The best part of life is

Despite failures and success

Life has the gift to go on

Making our lives awesome never a moment dull

Challenges are part of our lives

More than overcoming the thrills

We need to overcome the hesitation of facing it

Life is like a hand of cards

To be played with skills

You have to play the hand you are dealt with

Sometimes you must take chances to win

Just let go of the fear of going unheard

Today is the only day you are alive

Tomorrow never comes as it's said

Just follow your heart

Hate loud and love louder

Speak out your mind and heart without regrets

Don't get stuck with the thought what other people feel

Unfiltered emotions have the rawness of instincts

People who know you will never question

The others who don't know the real you will never understand

Doesn't matter

Stop being answerable

You are not a criminal

Feel blessed for the people around you have been fair

So what if that very person you have loved all your life

Has no clue why you love him

Your heart aches with the love you hold within

Think of it as a divine gift

That you have a heart that loves

Love fearlessly

Love unconditionally

Love faithfully as can be

Never have the feeling of being alone

For you are not the only one

You are not alone my friend

For half the world have loved and lived

Death is inevitable

But life is full of magic and tragic as it seems

Whether you choose magic or tragic is your heart's call

Nothing is perfect

No one wants something that's perfect out of fear unknown

Imperfection is what makes the world more adventurous

If you never cried

You wouldn't know the meaning of a smile

If you never loved

You wouldn't know a heart that aches

The penultimate moment of life

Keep following your heart till it finally stops to beat...thus Sonia speaks!

Alone I Shall Be

Growing up was so memorable

Everything was perfectly decorated

Living in a loved family with warmth

Not everyone's blessed as I was

Life moved on smoothly with worries kept aside

I loved my family for they were with me

Every time I was scared

They held me securely

With that trust I kept moving up and down life's ladder unseen

Little did I know

My life would end up in scatters

Now that I am fighting for the justice I never got

I have become a sore in the eye

The warmth somehow lost

The ones I took pride in

Nothing mattered more

Certainly have gone too far

For I can't see them anymore

For all these years that I have suffered

This was the last blow

When I thought they would stand by me

They had closed their doors

They couldn't see the way I have suffered and cried

All that I got in return were dialogues flying high

Someone said "it was your choice, keep me out of it"

And then the other one just blamed it all on me

I agree I have been at fault with the choices I had made

No one's perfect

Are you perfect let's see

When people have no excuses to make

They point out you are a liar

Only thing I have to say

Come light my funeral pyre

I have been hurt for so long

Now my heart has died inside

This mortal body that moves around was some day full of life

I was your family and your friend if you remember

Who would fight the world for you over and over again

Today for your fake honour and pride you are ashamed of me
quite right

Where was your pride and honour when I was beaten black
and blue

How could you see this happening and did not make a move

We are children of one clan which never distinguished

You were the one who taught me how to love unconditionally

You forgot what was taught to us

But I haven't forgotten it

I am proud

I am a survivor

Thanking, I am not like this

For God forbid if you were ever in trouble

I could kill for you

Unfortunately you overlooked the torment I went through

Every second of my life has been a turbulent scene

The best part was

When you blamed me without knowing the reality

What are you afraid of

I ask you now

How worse could it be

When your only aim is to make me look like a failure

As you please!

Wonder what else you need

Frankly I am not surprised

For I have been observing

The love and faith I had in you

Is now a distant dream

You failed me is all I can say

It sounds disturbing

Live my life I dare you

See the pain that I am in

For many years now I have been giving in

What will people say

Is the only thing I have been listening

I ask you who these people are

Please get them to me

I would love to see how they react when they are placed in my scene

It's easy preaching

Telling me this could have been better or that

But when you have gone through what I did

Trust me you can't match

Just because I keep silent

It's certainly not my cowardice

One thing life taught me

There's no one here for me

I am all by myself since

Everyone I love are gone

No one can be you

Hoping it was true

How insane was the poor me

Since I figured out in this world

Each to their own!

I will stand and fight with might and right till death defies
me

Even if it means there's no one next to me

I don't need fake people

Selfish souls fluttering around

I am alone

I shall fight alone

No one can stop me

One promise that I make to you

I will never call for help

You don't deserve to be my own

I am better off alone

I took my thoughts and framed it all

Alone I shall be and that will be all...thus Sonia speaks!

Nostalgia

I wish I were what I was

When I wished to be what I am

Life was so perfect when we were kids

No expectations, no time to think

Fun on the run it used to be

Playing around in a puddle of mud was cool you see

Those afternoons spent with a bunch of pals

Straight out of school

To climb up those trees with yummy fruits oh! Yeah

Our neighbours screaming

Shouting and losing their minds

Their afternoon nap was stolen by us on time

Our bunch of twenty and odd were too good to be true

The only thing in our minds was to have fun, that's true

The adversities of life had never taken a peep

Beauty of friendship knows no boundaries

We lived in different houses but our hub was one

From my home or someone's

Didn't matter at all

All of us together was the only thing that held importance

The best thing through the day was the ice-cream cart man

We bought four ice-creams and stole four more

Right away without a glance

No sense of guilt whatsoever

Trust me when I say I truly mean it

The ridiculous cricket we played in the yard

Fighting over not being out, well not bad

Those evenings when we played dumb charades

The boys had their group

And we girls always won

Our parents thinking over

We are all going to mess up

Fail in our exams or maybe fail in life that was to come

Telling them to chill

Assuring we would be fine

That was just an excuse to buy extra time

More time to play hide and seek

Running in the rain in the open field

Chilling near the river bed

Those crazy boat rides

I couldn't learn to swim out of fright

Today when I look back

It's so confining

We are all doing something meaningful with our lives

Not bad actually so far

My friends now are all over the world

Best part being we are all in touch

It's just that we are chasing life too fast

All of you my buddies from childhood I start

Catch the fresh air like I do

For you know life

It's unpredictable too

Well nostalgia is predefined

It's difficult to be nostalgic

When you can't remember your best times

It's awful when you find the present tensed days

And the past perfect makes all the sense

Nostalgia has taken over its best shape tonight

I so wish we could go back in time...thus Sonia speaks!

Achievement It Is

My conscious self and me

Had a long discussion when we were free

Isn't it enough to love someone

As far away as it can be

What's in a name

If I may say

The name itself has defamed us big way

I'm called a lover

A woman who's lost it all

And respects you

For being you

That's all I prefer my silence to hold my honour

For I'm not ashamed of being myself

It's true I tried to help you achieve your goals of pride

So you could succeed

Fact of the matter I'm in shackles

So you could walk scot free

That's all that matters

There goes my respect

Under your feet

So I allowed you to walk on me

I'm no one

Just an ordinary soul

But you mortal beings can't challenge my love

For it's extraordinary and pure

I gave up my dignity with pride

So all of you could talk about me

From being an honest woman of honour

To the day you put me out on the streets

I forgive you all

You unchallenged brains

For you can never see what I have seen

Material world to you

It belongs to self-pity and excuses you form

I'm acting blind

That's the least I could have done

The world will know your atrocities on me

How audacious can one be

Why am I not amazed at your kind

I have seen fools like you infinite times

And my heart feels sorry

For your fake existence

How interestingly intelligent people

You pose to be

The weirdest of things that you can speak

I ripped open my heart

Kept smiling with glee

Not a word to argue

Not a drop of tear to see

I would hate myself

If I compare you people and me

So I can see you all

Rejoicing at your achievements free

Alas! You got what you need

Let me give you a little piece of my mind

Can you stop me from feeling what I feel

What you missed out was I allowed you to think

I let you win

Cause I would have never seen you crying

I'm the one who lost her heart

I'm the one who knew "love" finally lasts

Love is not about achieving your goals

At times it's just good enough to let it go

If we talk about achievements here

Allow me to tell you the truth you fear

Bestowed with eternal love

My heart is with you

I love you through eternity

That's how it's going to be

Now on don't fear

As you know now

That's what achievement actually means to me...thus Sonia speaks!

Nobody's Fool

When you have seen life

From the closest of corners

Trying to decipher what's good and criminal

Seen it all yet have a mind of your own

When people take you for granted

And think they have won

You sit back smiling

Wondering is that all they have got

Your pain is someone's pleasure

You walk through that

Well, be proud

You gave a little work to the jobless retards

They actually thought they could break you down

You laugh out loud

Just by thinking what were the chances for them around

Practical living is what you believe in

Not magical romances intriguing

Funny some blokes have weird imaginings

They put you out there trying to pull a joke on you, well saddening

You keep mum

Just to see how immune you are to their advances

The last one is you to be affected

Rumours! Rumours doing the rounds

Always a punch bag in me

You have found

All one can do is take it easy

Let them talk

Let them be

You are the reason for their survival you see

Outstanding is the way how they pick on you

Best part being you already know what they are upto

Let them philander with their outrageous ways

Move unhindered with courage

Be brave

For these maggots do not mean a thing

You had so-called affairs

You didn't even know exist

It's ridiculous how they put your image out without guilt

Take a breath

Be calm and poised

You are not guilty

Let time do the talking

This world can wait to see

You don't have to stoop down to their levels underneath

Trust me you are so much better than the rest

Your life has more meaning to it

Minus the vagueness

The breed of fools will talk and brood about you

You are strong and unaffected

That's what you chose to do

Do your worst you limited brains

Go on take my name

I will have the last laugh after all the chaos ends

It can't get any worse

Can it?

Hope you got your moment of fame by demeaning me

One thing you should have remembered clearly

I have my prerogatives unlike you brainless wonders

I am nobody's fool

And certainly not a commoner...thus Sonia speaks!

Funny but True

Have you ever come across

A delusional fool with a brain loss

Well nothing to be surprised

Such people exist a bit too much around us

Sadistic pleasures they take on you

Bringing out your past

Playing with your pain

How jobless can one be

How mundane

No meaning in their lives indeed

For they just have one common aim

To embarrass you time and again

These foul souls have one bloody game

Ruin your day by blaming you lame

I have a couple of people just like these around

Doesn't really surprise me though

It was only expected out of them

Shameless to an extent they could go prancing for ages without shame

Taking your name for mere attention seeking and momentary
fame

Agony of it all being

They call themselves your kith and kin

What kind of insanity drives their nerves

To see you in trouble is in their vein

How sad is their life for I feel it's futile

No idea as to what they are doing to themselves

Well for starters you sick gossip mongers

Get a life! Trust me you need one

Sooner the better

Whatever were you thinking you desperate fools

I have been seeing so many like you

Hysterical is the word that best suits you

You couldn't ever differentiate between worth and waste

Yes you heard it right, you dimwit race

You are only mass minus the class

How pathetic is your inconsequential life

Wake up and see the light

If you don't understand the basic difference

Between silence and cowardice

I should have guessed you scattered brain weak

How could you ever understand silence is sane

Every time you stooped down with your unlimited defames

I kept silent cause I thought it was best

That was certainly not my cowardice

Believe me you

I mean this for real

What made you think I will stoop to your level at all

Well that's the basic difference in a lady and a mule

I am sure now you are searching for the meaning of a mule

That's what you are you hybrid fool

You really thought you could trap me with your sick tricks untrue

Good try I can say

But you failed miserably

I am a woman who stands by her words

What made you think you uncouth troupe

You could get away with anything you had woven

Sorry to say you twisted tribe

You really think I would have bought that

I can't stop myself from laughing at your decries

Spare me the detail

You are not my species

All I can say is grow up you fake frauds

It's funny but true

You are desperately hysterical

Don't you dare try your dirty skits on me

I will make sure I put you where you were always meant to be

How funny and how true

You need psychological help

Well, even God has taken his eyes off you

Only if you could see...thus Sonia speaks!

Unadulterated

Friendships develop over an extended period of time

Yet there are friendships which were there before we find

There are no rules to be friends

Then why do we think

If you are able to be yourself with one friend

It's a blessing

When we are together we share one mind

A crazier pair you will never find

Two people as different as Yin-Yang

Everything I am not, you are

We laugh, we cry and yet get back to see

Everything that's between us is worth believing

People say love comes and goes

I would beg to differ

Let the truth be known

For friendship is the only place where love breathes

Having you as my friend has elevated me

My friend such a bond I have never seen

You made me feel it's been there ever since

Your free spirited aura has made me see the light

I will cherish our friendship through the test of time

Through life and beyond I will stand by you

Our unadulterated friendship

Shall be there to speak through the history in line...thus Sonia speaks!

Perplexed

There have been people in this world

Perplexed to an extent not funny at all

They are confused not enigmatic

To see things simple is gigantic

Annoyingly scared to see the best in life

Competing in the game of catastrophic heights

Contemplating each time over

For little do they know

Deluded fantasies of their souls uproar

Exhausted ways of proving they are right

Makes me wonder

Why they are so out-dated

Is it related to inferiority complex or insanity after all?

Or is it cause of superior matches they follow?

Keeping it simple is all they need to do

But again everything for them is such a big deal

Well! Albeit it's their own audacity

Leave it right there or take it all with all certainty

One small suggestion

For you my perpetually perplexed friend

Confusion at its best is your real name

In your chase for one moment of fame

You lost all friends

Wonder what you gained

Once bitten twice shy

No one expects you to be precise

Why would I keep chasing your irrational goals

When you find none

You will know it all

It's ridiculous you haven't realised yet

You always get what you have given the rest

Hope one day you come out of it after all

I pity you my perplexed soul

That sums it up all...thus Sonia speaks!

Legitimate Hypocrites

A world full of fakes

Yes this is my take on the parasites so stale

They trick you into their world of false promises

You walk in the trap all delighted

You are human so you see them as one of you

What you failed to realise is none of it was true

With dreams of the future and finding a loving world

You find yourself in the midst of devils dressed as Gods

Well your dream world comes crashing down

When you see their true colours and background

It catapults your beautiful life from heaven to hell in one shoot

You try your best to fit in to this life untrue

Then you find yourself trapped in the pathetic grip

These so-called humans could come in any form

If at all one could figure out in the quest of it all

You find yourself suffering for things you have never done

Beaten black and blue has become your fate soon

These monsters just move about in the social circle at large

Making humans wonder they are the best as well in form

You try to hide your tears so your peers don't see your pain

More power to those monsters is all you have gained

Typical society is where you belong

Does it matter you are a woman of substance at all

Anguished with your state you cry alone

One fine day you wake up to take that real final call

When you take a stand for not taking this pain anymore

Shockingly your peers ask you whether it's true after all

You belong to a class where in everything is perfect

How could you suffer is the question from one and all

You were provided with everything that you always required

And you wake up to this with utter surprise

Is being materialistic the basic prerequisite

Is there no one in this world who would come forward to heal

The tormented soul

The heart that bleeds

When you find it nowhere

You rise above it

All by yourself you have learnt it the hard way

Living life with dignity is all you will need at bay

My friend you are one of the few who have seen the worse

Yet managed to remain sane amidst all this chaos

Legitimate hypocrites of this world

Yes legitimate hypocrites is the name for these losers

These boastful pompous fools belong to the gutters

For all the women and men in this world

If you ever come across such legitimate hypocrites

Just make sure you show those losers your front door...thus Sonia speaks!

Seize the Day

My power today

Lies in seizing the day

I step in to recognise or create new goals and ways

To take it to the next level and being there

I am empowered to rise to the occasion

Beyond hypocrisy and superstition

I found a solution

By a window of goodwill

I transform through motivation

This could be a time for self-evaluation

I feel the need to prove myself through resurrection

So I put my best foot forward

And double check my condition

Or do something more interestingly in a different direction

I am clear about my intentions

Let my soul be free and express what I need

Considering a more serious commitment

My power today lies in completion

I celebrate and am grateful for captured moments of simple perfection

Satisfy my heart's connectivity in juxtaposition

I seek happiness I see in abundance

Gives me confidence to take it to the next level of ramifications

We made it

"Unconditional love makes us we"

Give us a home where the heart is

End of it all

I am not alone

I am empowered by gratitude and sheer affection

Our virtue is emotional fulfilment and realisation

There is nothing more romantically isolating

than self-righteous indignation

Blind trust, demanding proof of love

A victim of jealousy or a desire for vengeance

Unless it is the inability to get the connection

Between your convictions and your belief system

And the natural eventualities

It's hard to believe

But one thing life taught us for sure

You get what you give in return

Hence seize the day before it's gone...thus Sonia speaks!

Hope vs Hopelessness

Hope springs spreading its wide wings

Making me count my days in grief

Hopelessness takes the front seat

Asking me not to wish

You are in pain so am I

Nothing is moving

Hope knocks in time

And again asking me to wait

I know I have to wait

To finally see what's in the making

Don't judge me with my flaws

Everyone has their shortcomings

It had never really been my priority

This hopeless feeling of losing

Can't tell you what I am going through

Every moment regretting

Wish I never judged you that way

Never could believe that it's happening

The heart that I hurt was screaming

Not your words

Your silence was out shouting

Why is it that we fail to understand

It's not the end but the beginning

Hoping you would know someday

Praying hopelessly for your well-being

I can't see you hurt and in pain

There is nothing I am rejoicing

Explains what I feel for you

Never knew that this was coming

I blamed you for reasons unknown

The situation was demanding

If staying away from you is all I get

Then that's the way of your reasoning

What do I do with my hopeless heart

Hoping beyond hope

It's dreaming

How could I be so insensible

Hope I would have asked you first before concluding

Now that I am at fault, there is no point pondering

In the process I lost my only love

My heart and mind are struggling

Should have known from day one

You would never do anything to hurt me even in your dreams

I have nothing to complain

As it was me who did the wrong doing

Hoping you will forgive me

Hopelessly waiting for your healing

I am sorry my love is all I can say

Can't tell you with what am dealing

Hope versus hopelessness is not just a feeling...thus Sonia speaks!

Deaf to the World

When you are feisty and wild

Looking at the world and its ridiculous ties

Where truth becomes a faint cry

The book of lies is the only sight

You try and wake the pretentious fools

The feeling is mutual

To the loner group

Point of view is just the same

The loners are silent

Cause they have seen the game

You soon realise why they are quiet

They have tried to wake the world outside

Fell silent

No one could hear them call

You scream and cry for a soul to see

No one feels

The way you feel

Don't stand there thinking

Why you

There have been plenty

Long before you

It's just that you gave your best

The others just left

Before the test

You find yourself standing

At your loneliest best

Outrageously feeling foolish

For no damn jest

Be kind to yourself

You are a fighter after all

The people who lost you were born losers

Nobody defines you

Only you have the pleasure

To judge your ways

As to why you are right

When the tides were high

You took control of life

Spoke your heart in dire circumstances

On a roll you are a woman of substance

Take charge

Win it or leave it all

You have your chance

When the world speaks about you in different hues

Laugh, dance, sing and love it through

That's exactly the difference between you and them

Deaf to the world

You rise again...thus Sonia speaks!